Thomas Allibone Janvier

Color Studies and a Mexican Campaign

Thomas Allibone Janvier

Color Studies and a Mexican Campaign

ISBN/EAN: 9783337422844

Printed in Europe, USA, Canada, Australia, Japan

Cover: Foto ©Andreas Hilbeck / pixelio.de

More available books at **www.hansebooks.com**

COLOR STUDIES

AND

A MEXICAN CAMPAIGN

BY

THOMAS A. JANVIER

AUTHOR OF "THE AZTEC TREASURE-HOUSE," "STORIES OF OLD NEW
SPAIN," "THE MEXICAN GUIDE," ETC.

NEW YORK
CHARLES SCRIBNER'S SONS
1899

TROW'S
PRINTING AND BOOKBINDING COMPANY
NEW YORK.

To

C. A. J.

OUT OF WHOSE COLOR-BOX THESE STORIES CAME,

AND TO WHOSE SUGGESTIONS THE BEST PORTIONS

OF ONE OF THESE STORIES,

"JAUNE D'ANTIMOINE,"

ARE DUE.

There is no Moral in this book,
No Purpose is there 'twixt its covers.
In truth, whichever way you look
You'll only find—a Pair of Lovers.

COLOR STUDIES.

ROSE MADDER.

OLD MADDER lived on the top floor of an artist rookery down in the Greenwich region—near enough to the Tenth Street Studio Building for him to say that he lived in an artistic quarter of the town ; under the roof, as he was wont very reasonably to explain, because that was the only place in any house where a man could get a sky light. Catch him spoiling good painting by working by a side light, he would say.

A dozen or more other men, all painters, had quarters in the building. Some of them were old fellows—old Cremnitz White and Robert Lake, for instance—who had been painting atrociously all their lives, and who all the while had sincerely believed themselves to be the greatest artists of the age, whom fate, and the public's bad taste, and all the malign forces at work in the world (but their own incapacity), had united to trample on. And with these there were some young fellows— Vandyke Brown, little Sap Green, Jaune d'Antimoine, McGilp, and two or three more—who had not worked long enough to prove very conclusively whether their work was bad intrinsically or bad only because they had yet a good deal to learn. All of these men snarled and snapped at each other more or less, and abused each other's work, and envied each other's (apparently) less bad fortune ; and, on the whole, were pretty good friends.

Of them all, old Madder was the only one who had his family with him : and old Madder's family consisted solely and simply of his daughter Rose. In all Greenwich there was not a more charming little body than Rose Madder ; probably it would be within bounds to say that there was not a more charming little body in all New York. She was twenty or thereabouts, and as plump as a little partridge, and as good-humored as the day was long. You must have seen her face—at least as good a copy of it as old Madder could make, which is not saying a great deal, to be sure—a dozen times in the last dozen years at the Academy exhibitions; for Madder was an N. A., and so was one of those whose "line" privileges make the Academy exhibitions so hopelessly exasperating. Rose began to do duty as a model before she was weaned ("Soldier's Widow and Orphaned Child," Rubens Madder, A. N. A., 1864), but the first really recognizable portrait of her that saw the light was "The Bread-winner" (1875), in which she figured in an apron, with rolled-up sleeves, making real bread at what a theatrical person would call a practicable table. Since then she had gone to the Academy regularly every year—excepting that sad year when her mother died, and old Madder had not the heart to finish his "Dress-Making at

Home," nor to do anything at all save mourn the loss that never could be repaired.

It was generally believed that the reason why Madder's pictures sold—for some of them did sell—was that Rose, even badly painted, was worth buying. All his friends wanted to borrow her, but Madder would never lend her : she was too valuable to him as stock-in-trade. And with the odd hundreds which dropped in from his pictures, with some other odd hundreds that he picked up by painting portaits—things hard as stones, which he was wont to say, modestly, were good because he had caught completely the style of his old master, Sully —he managed to pick up a living, and to keep the frame-maker from the door.

It was the prettiest sight in the world to see Rose posing for her father. She had seen too many pictures, and had heard too much picture-talk, not to know that her father's pictures were pretty bad. But she loved her father with all her heart, and she would have died cheerfully rather than let him for a single moment suspect that she did not truly believe him to be the greatest artist of his own or any previous age. And Madder, while yet recognizing the fact that some few men had excelled him in art, found much solace for his soul in his daughter's unlimited admiration of his greatness. Therefore, when she posed for him, and with much gravity discussed with him how the pose would have been arranged by his great name-sake, Rubens (in point of fact, Reuben was the name given him by his godfathers and godmothers in baptism) or Sir Joshua or some other of his acknowledged superiors, and all the while talked heartening talk to him, and gave him—with due deference to the interests of the pose—sweet looks of love out of her gentle blue eyes; when all this was going on, it was, I repeat, the prettiest sight in the world.

Vandyke Brown thought so, certainly; and that he might enjoy it freely, he made all manner of excuses for coming into Madder's studio while work was going on. The

most unblushing of all these excuses—
though the one that he found most useful—
was that he wanted to study Madder's style.
This was carrying mendacity to a very high
pitch indeed, for until within the past year,
Brown had been accustomed to cite Madder's style as being a most shining example
of all that was pernicious in the old school.
Brown was a League man, of course, and
held the Academy in an exceeding great
contempt.   Yet now, for hours at a stretch—
and when he had work of his own on hand
that needed prompt attention—he would sit
by old Madder's easel and talk high art with
him, and listen calmly to the utterance of
old-time heresies fit to make your flesh
creep, and hear for the hundredth time Madder draw the parallel between himself and
poor old Ben Haydon, and, worst of all,
watch old Madder placidly painting away in
a fashion that sent cold creeps down his
(Brown's) back, and made him long to take
Madder by the shoulders and ram his head
through the canvas.   All this torment Van-

dyke Brown would undergo for no better reason than that Rose Madder was a dozen feet away on the platform, and by thus sitting by her father's side he had the joy of hearing her sweet voice and the greater joy of seeing her sweeter smiles.

What was still more unreasonable in Brown's conduct was his sturdy objection to sharing this mixed pleasure with anybody else. When little Sap Green came in, as he very often did, he would fume and fret, and make himself so disagreeable to the little man—who was a good enough little chap in his way, guilty of no other sin than of painting most abominably—that Rose would have to intervene with all her tact and gentleness to prevent a regular outbreak. And it was still worse when the visitor was McGilp. Brown hated this sleek, slippery person most heartily. He hated his always-smooth, reddish-yellow hair; he hated the oily smoothness of his voice; he hated his silent, cat-like ways; and, most of all, he hated him for his insolence in venturing to love Rose.

Moreover, McGilp was Brown's rival in art.   He was a League man too, and at the life-class his studies were the only ones which gave Brown any real uneasiness.   Their styles were different, but there was very little choice in the quality of their work. And as each would have been the acknowledged first if the other had been out of the way, there was not much love lost between them.   To do Brown justice, though, mere professional rivalry never would have set him at loggerheads with anybody; it was the other rivalry that made him hate McGilp —coupled with a profound conviction that in McGilp's composition there was a thoroughly bad streak that by rights should bar completely his pretensions to Rose's love.

An ugly piece of work had been done at the life-class in the past season, that never yet had received a satisfactory explanation. The pose was a strong one, and both Brown and McGilp had worked hard over it—with Brown ahead.   On the morning of the last day of the pose Brown had found his study most ingeniously ruined.   It was not painted out, but here and there over the whole of it bits had been touched in that took out all its strength, and reduced it simply to the level of the commonplace.   The study was spoiled but so cleverly that even the men who had watched Brown at his work were inclined to believe—in accordance with the humane custom that makes all of us give a man in a tight place the benefit of every doubt that will make his place tighter—that they had overestimated its merits, and that the study had been weak from the start.   Brown believed most thoroughly—though with no more material ground for his belief than the skill with which the changes had been made, and a vague remembrance of seeing McGilp still pottering over his work after the class broke up the day before—that McGilp was the man who had played this scurvy trick on him.   He kept his suspicions to himself; but, since he held them, it is no great wonder that when McGilp was the intruder upon his lounging in old Madder's studio, Rose needed all her cleverness in order to stave off a storm !

The fact of the matter was that Brown was desperately in love with Rose, and as yet was in a state of anything but pleasing uncertainty as to whether there was the least chance in the world that his love would be returned. What made his situation all the more uncomfortable was his profound conviction—at least in his lucid intervals—that for him to fall in love with anybody was a most serious piece of folly. For all in the world that he had to live upon was the very doubtful—save that it certainly always was insufficient—income that he made by scrapwork for the illustrated papers, with now and then an extra lift when a sanguine dealer was weak enough to buy one of his little pictures. He had shown this much good sense, at least ; he never yet had tried to paint a big one. He did believe, and he had some ground for believing, that after a while he might do work that would be worth something. In the meantime he sailed close to the wind, and had anything but an easy time of it.

But God tempers the wind to the shorn lamb, down Greenwich way. In that modest region one may get a very filling breakfast for twenty cents, and for thirty cents a dinner; and Brown was a rare hand at making coffee wherewith to mitigate the severity of his early morning loaf of bread. And, on the whole, he did not find this hand-to-mouth sort of life especially uncomfortable. But he had wisdom enough to perceive that, without something more assured in the way of a living, getting married was a risky undertaking. To be sure, he had " prospects." His uncle Mangan, who was a highly respected leather man down in the Swamp, had neither wife nor child, and Brown felt tolerably certain that some day or other a fair share of the profits of his uncle's leather business would be his. But Uncle Mangan was a tough, cheery, hearty old fellow, who very well might live to be a hundred; at which time his nephew would be five-and-seventy.   The thought of an engagement of fifty years' duration, ending in a marriage at three-score years and fifteen, was rather appalling.

" 'E is what you call rofe, very rofe, my friend, such long time of waiting for the love," observed Jaune d'Antimoine, sympathizingly, when, as his custom was at short intervals, Brown had relieved his mind by confiding his hopes and expectations and doubts to his friend.

"Rough! I should rather think so! If you knew how rough it was, you'd wonder that I don't end it all by jumping into the river!"

"Ah! but you forget, my poor Brown. I also 'ave my rose that for I long, my sweet Rose Carthame ; I also am most 'opeless and most meeserable. And I am even more meeserable than you, for 'ave I not one wretched rival—that most execrable countryman of mine, which calls 'imself the count —count ! parbleu ! 'e is no count—Siccatif de Courtray ? I—I vill yet eat 'im alive, vig and all !"

It will be observed that Brown withheld from his friend his conviction that he also had a rival in McGilp. Brown did not like to admit this fact even to himself. To couple this man, even in his thoughts, with Rose, seemed to him nothing short of an outrageous insult. That Rose had any other feeling than that of toleration for McGilp he could not, he would not, believe ; but he knew that it was useless to close his eyes to the truth that McGilp was in love with Rose, and was bent upon winning her, and that McGilp was not the sort of man to abandon lightly anything that he had fully made up his mind to do. He was a rival ; and, in that he possessed force of character that begot persistency of purpose, he was a dangerous rival. So Brown was in a melancholy way over it all — trying to nerve himself to faith in his success in art ; trying to hope that Rose, too, would have faith in him ; trying not to fall into the habit of thinking what pleasant things might happen should his uncle Mangan suddenly be called into another and a better world.

" I SAY, old man, are you going in for the Philadelphia prizes ? " asked little Sap Green, as he tipped a lot of life-studies off a chair in Brown's studio, sat down on the chair, and blew such clouds of cigarette smoke that presently his face shone out through the mist like that of a spectacled cherub.

"I do wish to heaven, Green, that you wouldn't smoke those vile things in here. If smoking a pipe like a Christian makes you sick, then don't smoke anything."

" I am," Green continued. " Of course, I know that I don't stand a first chance, for there are several men who can paint better that I can. Somebody else will get the three thousand dollars, I suppose ; but I don't see why I shouldn't get one of the medals. Even the bronze would be worth having. It does a fellow a heap of good in the cata-logues, you know, to have a medal after his name."

" And you might wear it round your neck on a string. But I don't think that you need a bronze medal, Sap ; you've enough of the article already for all practical purposes."

" Don't joke about it, Brown. I'm quite serious. You see, I have an idea. Don't whistle that way, it's rude. You've been associating too much with the boys who hang around Jefferson Market. Yes, I have an idea that I think is bound to win. I'm going to do the ' Surrender at Yorktown.' You know I'm pretty good all around—figures, animals, landscape, and marine. The trouble is to get a subject, inside the conditions, that will bring them all in. ' Yorktown ' is just the card. Figures of George and Cornwallis—or whoever the other fellow was—in foreground; staff in middle distance ; group of cavalry close up in front on right; French ships close up in front on left ; lots of landscape, with tents and masses of troops in background. There you have it ; and if that don't take a medal, it will be because the committee has not the sense to know a good picture when it has one under its nose."

"True," observed Brown, thoughtfully. "What a lucky thing it is for you, Sappy, that Trumbull didn't take out a copyright; or, if he did, that it has expired by limitation."

"Trumbull, indeed! It's just because Trumbull made such a mess of that subject that I want to show how it ought to be painted. Do you know, Brown, I think that this is the very end that old Temple has in view. He wants these grand subjects, which were ruined in our fathers' and grandfathers' time, to be taken up by the men of the New School and painted properly. But I do wish that the Philadelphia people had not made this absurd rule about size. What is a man to do with such a subject as the 'Surrender at Yorktown' on a beggarly eight-by-ten-foot canvas?"

"You can get an awful lot of paint on a canvas that big, Sap."

"You are a beast, Brown. When a man

comes to you, really in earnest, to tell you of his aspirations and hopes, you answer him simply with low chaff. You haven't a scrap of the real artist feeling in your whole composition." And Sap Green flounced out of the studio, leaving Brown grinning at him.

But Brown was more in earnest than he had cared to own. He had been thinking very seriously about the Philadelphia prizes, and he had made up his mind to go in for them. He knew that he had no more chance than little Sap Green had for the great prize; but he also knew, just as Sap knew, that even the lowest of the three medals was worth very earnest striving after. In winning it there was honor to be gained, and there was money to be made—for there was not much doubt but that a medalled picture would find a purchaser—and honor and money were what he longed for just then with all his heart; for these were the means that would compass the end that he lived for —Rose.

And Brown also had an idea. It was not

as big an idea, in square feet, as Sap's ; but it possessed the advantages of having something of originality about it, and of being within the scope of his ability. He had the color-study pretty well in shape already, and he believed that he had a good thing. It was a simple picture, and very much inside the eight-by-ten-foot limitation. The scene was a roadway in a dark wood, the foreground in deepest shadow. Out beneath the arching branches was seen a misty valley, shimmering in the cool, crisp light of early day, the nearly level sunbeams striking brilliantly upon the white tents of a camp. And seen under the bowering trees, but a little beyond them, and in the full brightness of the morning light, was a single figure, brought into strong relief against the dark hills lying in shadow on the valley's farther side. The figure was that of a woman in Quaker dress—the soft brown and gray of her shawl and gown in tone with the deeper browns and grays of the foreground and of the misty valley beyond; a good high-light in the white kerchief folded across her breast. She was kneeling. Her shawl had fallen back, showing her beautiful head and face—beautiful with the beauty not of youth, but of serene holiness—on which the sun shone full. Her eyes, moist with tears, were full of a glad thankfulness, and through all the lines of the face and figure was an expression of great joy, humbled by devout gratitude to Him who had brought her safely to her journey's end, and so had given her the victory. The title, "Saving Washington's Camp at Whitemarsh," gave the key to the story : the woman was Lydia Darragh, who went out from Philadelphia, and gave the warning that enabled the Continental army to repulse the assault planned by General Howe. And Brown was determined to work on this picture as he never had worked before.

Naturally, McGilp was not asleep in regard to the Philadelphia competition ; and he also had his mind set on winning a medal—and with it, Rose. His picture was more striking than Brown's, but infinitely less pretentious than Sap Green's stupendous "Yorktown." It was called "Raising the Flag at Stony Point," and in its way it was an uncommonly good thing. The time, as in Brown's picture, was sunrise—the sunrise following the night of General Wayne's gallant assault. In the immediate front of the picture was water, tumbling in little waves which sparkled in the sunlight; and from this rose sharply the rocky bank, and sheer above the bank an angle of the fort. Standing on the parapet, in crisp relief against the green-blue sky, was "Mad Anthony" himself, in the act of running up the Continental flag; while at his feet a mass of red upon the gray stones of the parapet, and throwing a rich crimson reflection down upon the broken water below, was the flag of the conquered foe. Over the whole picture was a flood of strong, clear light that emphasized the spirited action and elate pose of the single figure: it was a stirring story of a gallant fight crowned by a well-won victory. Except that the values of the lights and shades were about the same in both, McGilp's and Brown's pictures had absolutely nothing in common; and while Brown's had the advantage in earnestness and depth of poetic feeling, McGilp's, being bold and aggressive, was much more likely to hit the popular taste.

It was known presently among the artists that both men had entered in the Philadelphia race; but while McGilp made no secret of his "Stony Point," Brown absolutely refused to let his subject be known. He kept his door locked, and the few men whom he admitted now and then saw no more of his work than the curtain that hung over it, jealously.

Not a word passed between Brown and McGilp as to what would be the result should either of them win a medal, but each man knew what the other was working for, and each felt that the other's success meant his own defeat. Not that Brown believed that McGilp ever could win Rose, for he loved

Rose himself too much to fancy, even for a moment, that she could love McGilp under any circumstances; but he felt that unless there was enough good in himself to enable him to take one of the three medals, his career as an artist might as well come definitely to an end, and his love for Rose with it. McGilp, who was cool-headed enough to see in what direction Rose's inclinations were tending, believed that in his own success, coupled with Brown's failure, rested his only chance of having Rose so much as listen to him. Therefore, both men went at their work with all their strength, and put into it their whole hearts.

Now Brown was a good deal laughed at for making such a mystery about his picture; but he knew what he was about, and the laughing did not at all discomfit him. His purpose was a diplomatic one: that he might have a secret in common with Rose. He knew enough of the theory and practice of love-making to know that a bond of this sort counted for a good deal.

As soon as the picture was fairly in his head, he decided that Rose, and Rose alone, should know all about it. So, when he met her coming home from Jefferson Market one morning, he turned back to carry her market-basket, and to tell her the secret that he intended should be his first parallel. And he made such quick work of it that the secret was in her keeping before they had passed the pretty little triangular park where Grove Street and Christopher Street slant into each other. Rose now never looks un·der the archway formed by the trees in the little park, and the elm and willow on the sidewalk, that she does not fancy that she sees Lydia Darragh kneeling there, while Grove Street and Christopher Street beyond widen out into the tent-dotted valley of Whitemarsh.

Having told this secret, Brown had to steady himself sharply that he might not tell the other secret that lay on the very end of his tongue—how all his hope of the prize really was hope of Rose herself. Possibly

Rose had a feeling sense of what he was trying not to tell, for she talked so much about
the picture that he had no chance to talk
about anything else. And she was as sympathetic as even Brown—who wanted a good
deal of sympathy—could desire.

After that Brown managed pretty often to
meet Rose as she came from market; and
Rose did not resent the persistent frequency
of these purely chance encounters. She reasoned with herself that it must be a great
comfort to him to have anybody to talk with
about his work and hopes, and that for her
to refuse to listen to him, since he had happened to make her his confidante, would be
exceedingly ungracious, to say the least of
it; which reasoning, if a trifle too general in
its premises, certainly was sound in its con-
clusions. And by good generalship she always managed that his other secret should
remain untold—though as the days went by
she found this to be an increasingly difficult
task, that constantly called for more vigorous
defensive tactics. And what still further

complicated matters was that Rose grew less and less disposed to use defensive tactics at all.

Brown put in honest work on his picture. He spent a couple of days in getting his studies on the border of the Whitemarsh valley; and he got up morning after morning at unconscionable hours, so as to be in the Park at sunrise to study effects of early morning light—and mighty puzzling he found them! Luckily, his sister, Verona, was the type that he needed for Lydia Darragh, and she posed for him with all the good-will in the world; and nobody knows what a deal of good-will is required in posing until after trying it for a while.

Under Verona's protection, Rose saw the picture now and then, and so was able to talk about it considerately with Brown in the course of their walks. And these walks came to be a good deal prolonged; for Brown developed a notable tendency for taking the wrong turns when they were going home, so that when they thought they were in Grove Street, they suddenly would find themselves drifting down on Abingdon Place. After all, though, these mistakes were not unnatural, when you come to think what a desperately crooked region Greenwich is. That people should go astray in a part of the town so hopelessly topsy-turvy, that in it Fourth Street crosses Tenth Street at right angles, need not be a matter for surprise. What was a little surprising, though, was that it did not occur to Rose that inasmuch as Verona now knew all about the picture, Brown no longer stood in very urgent need of herself as a confidante. But it certainly is a fact that this view of the situation never once crossed her mind.

McGilp's " Stony Point," meanwhile, was getting along pretty well, too. The man had a great deal of facility, and more than a fair allowance of talent ; and he never had worked so hard as he was working now. Little Sap Green, who had a great fondness for knowing all that was going on, paid frequent visits to his studio, and volunteered statements of the results of his observations to Brown :

"It's not as good as ' Yorktown,' of course, but it's a mighty good picture, Van. He's got in his lights and shades in a way that I don't believe I could improve on myself, and there's lots of tremendous color, and the figure is as strong as a house. He's booked for a medal as sure as I am ; and I do hope, old man, that this thing of yours you're so dark about will get the third. Of course, you know, Brown, that I don't a bit like having to run my work against yours in this way. But I can't help it, you know; and I hope that if I win, and you don't, you wont have any ill-feeling about it. And, I say, Brown, what are you going to do about a frame ? I've been to see Keyes & Stretcher, and the brutes absolutely refuse to let me have one unless I pay cash down ; and for a ten-by-eight they want eighty dollars. They might as well ask me to pony up a thousand ! I offered Keyes a lien on the picture, and he had the indecency to say that the security undoubtedly was big enough, but it wasn't marketable. Do you know, I'm half sorry I didn't paint ' Washington on his Death-bed ' on a forty-by-sixty? I've got a forty-by-sixty frame on my ' Hector at the Gates of Troy,' and I might just as well have saved money by using it over again."

So the summer drifted along pleasantly, and Brown's picture daily came nearer to being what he wanted it to be. He knew, of course, that he never could realize his ideal, but he also knew that his picture was intrinsically good. It was a long way ahead of anything that he had ever done. Verona, who was not a bad judge of a picture, approved it; and, what was more to the purpose, so did Rose. By the end of August it practically was finished, leaving him a fortnight and more for that delicate operation known as " going all over it "—in the course of which many a capital picture is hopelessly spoiled.

Brown did not know, when he got up at four o'clock, on the morning of the 28th of August, to go out to the Park for a final study of the effects of early sunlight, that the most eventful day of his life had come ; but it had. He was in such a hurry to get to the Park before the sun rose, that he went without his coffee, contenting himself with munching a bit of bread as he walked from the Sixth Avenue entrance along the shadowy paths in the fresh coolness of the early day. Therefore it came to pass that when his observations were ended—with the satisfactory result of showing him that the thing he was in doubt about was right—he was aroused to the fact that he was most prodigiously hungry. And, being in a hopeful frame of mind, he decided promptly that he would spend the full value of a half-dollar in getting a good breakfast at the Hungaria, before going home to his work. Not exactly a headlong extravagance this, yet having in it enough of extravagance to give to the breakfast an agreeable spice of adventure.

It was a good while after eight o'clock when he got home ; yet, notwithstanding the lateness of the hour, he began the ascent of the stairs leisurely, and with the air of a man, who, having breakfasted well, is contented with himself and all the world. But at the third step his movements suddenly were vastly accelerated. From one of the floors above him sounded a scream and a cry for help—and the voice crying for help was the voice of his Rose!

He went up the steps three at a time, hearing as he went yet more screams, and the sound of opening doors, and of hurrying feet, which showed that everybody in the building was aroused. And when he got to the fourth floor he found that his own studio was the centre of the commotion—and a pretty kettle of fish he found there! The easel, with Lydia Darragh upon it, was lying flat upon the floor, and in front of it—looking, as he has since told her, like a delightful blue-eyed enraged lioness defending her cubs—was Rose. She had her big pie-making apron on, and her sleeves were rolled up, and she had dabs of flour all over her (for the life of him he could not keep a grinning recollection of her father's horrible "Bread-winner" out of his mind), and in one of her beautiful, plump arms was a red gash, and all her lovely arm was bloody, and there was blood upon her floury apron and on the floor. A little on one side was old Cremnitz White—he was a big old fellow, with lots of strength left in him—with his hand twisted so tight in McGilp's collar that McGilp's sleek face was growing purple, and his eyes were protruding ominously ; and old Cremnitz's long gray beard was fairly wagging with righteous rage. Madder was doing his best to make Cremnitz let go—for the life was being choked out of McGilp rapidly—and little Sap Green was dancing around the room in a perfect whirl of excitement, and saying at every step, " Oh, dear !" Three or four other men entered the room at Brown's heels, and stopped just inside the doorway, in wonder of what the dickens it all could mean.

It was not a time for standing on ceremony. Brown had Rose in his arms in a moment.

" My darling ! What has happened ?"

And for answer Rose threw her arms around his neck (the coat with the blood-stain on the left shoulder he will cherish to his dying day), and laid her head down on his breast, and sobbed forth :

" He — the wicked villain ! Oh ! he's ruined it. But—but, indeed, I did my best to stop him. To think of poor, dear Lydia Darragh with her two lovely eyes poked out, and the rest of her all cut to pieces ! Oh, the wretch ! Please, *please* let Mr. White choke him, papa. But no matter if you have lost the medal, dear, you—you shall have *me* all the same. For I love you with all my heart, and I hate him, and I always have hated him. There ! " (From which utterance, especially from that part of it relating to herself and the medals, the inference is a fair one that Verona Brown had chatterboxed away her brother's secret to Rose, so that for ever so long it had been no secret at all !)

" Now, sir ! What have you got to say

for yourself?" asked old Madder, sternly. He had managed to drag Cremnitz off by this time, and McGilp stood in one corner of the room gasping and rubbing his throat with his hand. (It was a month and more before he could swallow anything without a painful reminder of the exceeding boniness of Cremnitz's knuckles.)

"Nothing that will do any good. I'm beaten, among you all, and that's the end of it. But I will say this, though: I didn't mean to cut Brown's picture when I came in here. I didn't mean to come in here at all. He went out in a hurry, I suppose, for as I came along the passage I found his door open. I knew that he had gone out, for he waked me up with his confounded noise, and I had heard him go down-stairs. So I knew that he couldn't stop me, and I came in to see his picture. When I found that it was better than mine—for it was better, a good deal better—I couldn't help what I did. I knew that if either of us got one of the Philadelphia medals, it would not be me;

and I knew what that meant for both of us. You don't know what it would have meant, and I don't intend to tell you. I got into a rage over it all, and the first thing that I knew I had picked up his palette-knife, and had run it through the picture a dozen times. Then she came down-stairs, and saw me through the open door, and what I was doing, and came in and tried to stop me. I was nearly crazy, I suppose, for I fought with her, and somehow she got that cut in her arm. I don't imagine that any of you, even now, think that I cut her on purpose. Then White came in and grabbed me, and the rest of you after him, and you know what happened better than I do, for he came precious near to murdering me.

"And, now, what are you going to do with me? Take me around to the Jefferson Market Police Court, and charge me with aggravated assault and battery? You can do it if you want to. You are on top."

There was a rather awkward pause after this direct question. Certainly, the course that McGilp suggested was the proper one to take ; but nobody, except Cremnitz White, wanted to take it. For bringing Rose into a police court, and her name into the newspapers, was not to be thought of. And so, when Rose—her father had washed her arm in Brown's basin, and had let Brown help him, and they were tying up the cut in clean paint-rags—said to let him go, everybody but Cremnitz felt relieved.

Half swaggering, half slinking, McGilp went out of the room ; and enough decency remained in him to make him leave town forthwith. His unfinished "Stony Point" went with him. Presumably, he did not complete it, for when the Philadelphia exhibition opened it was not there. As he went down the stairs, Cremnitz White looked reproachfully at Madder, and exclaimed :

" Ach, mein Gott, Madter ! Fhy dit yoo shoost not let me shoke him, and pe done mit it ? For him shoking woult haf been most goot—most goot inteed ! "

So "Saving Washington's Camp at White-marsh " never entered into the Philadelphia competition at all. It was not, to be sure, quite so badly cut up as Rose in her excitement had declared it to be ; but it was so far gone that exhibiting it in public was not to be thought of. However, there was a private exhibition of it the next day in Brown's studio, that bore better fruit than if it had gone to Philadelphia, and had taken the three-thousand-dollar Temple prize.

The organizer of this exhibition was Verona, and the unit who attended it was Mr. Mangan Brown. Verona, as has already been hinted, had rather a faculty for telling things, and immediately after the catastrophe had become known to her she set off valorously for the Swamp, sought out Uncle Mangan among his kips and hides, and told him precisely what had happened to his nephew, and begged him to come up and look at the picture, with the wreck of which, seemingly, everything had been lost. Then she vigorously urged her brother to make

Lydia Darragh as presentable as possible, with careful gumming of linen on the back, and with touches of paint on the ragged edges of cut canvas; and her urging was not wholly unsuccessful. The picture was a sad object still, but enough of its beauty and worth remained to convince even a very skeptical person that the man who had painted it had a right to make a profession of art. And Uncle Mangan, who until then had been as skeptical as he well could be in regard to his nephew's self-elected vocation, saw it and was convinced.

"I have always thought, Van, that you were a fool," said Uncle Mangan, with a cheerful frankness and a most evident sincerity. "But now I think that the fool of the family has been quite a different person. So the big prize, the one that you didn't expect to get, is three thousand dollars? Well, you just *shall* get it, as soon as I can go down town and write the check. But you must paint the picture over again, for I want it. It's the most beautiful thing that

I ever saw, by gad! And the directors of
our bank last week voted five hundred dollars to have my portrait painted, to go with
the set of presidents, and you shall do that
too. And I always have wanted a portrait
of your aunt Caledonia, the only sister I
have in the world, and you shall do that.
And my partner, Gamboge, said only the
other day that he wanted some pictures for
his new house, and you shall do those. And
we want two or three pictures for the new
room at the club, and you shall do one of
them. And—and I'll make it my business,
Van, to see that you have all the work you
want as long as I live ; and when I die you'll
find that you can work or not, just as you
please, my boy. And I'm proud of you,
Van, for the way in which you've worked
along all these years without a scrap of encouragement from those who ought to have
encouraged you most. And I'm ashamed
of myself for the way in which I've stood off,
like a regular priest and Levite, from my
own dead brother Cappagh's son.

"And now where's this little girl who fought and bled for you like such a regular heroine ? For she will be a Brown, too, before long, and I want to give her the kiss that I have a right to give her ; and that— God bless her !—she shall have with all my heart !"

" THAT I will be the best man of you, my dear Brown, you know well would be to me much joy. But perceive !" and Jaune d'Antimoine slowly turned himself about, that the worst might be known of the many shabbinesses of his very ancient suit of clothes. " And these are beyond all the best that I do own of all the world, my Brown. What would you 'ave ? For your wedding, in such clothings as these, I should be one 'orror; one—I do not know the English— one *épouvantail*. And in the small month that does pass before your wedding comes, what can be for me to do that such vast moneys as must be paid for new clothings shall be mine ? No, my good friend, 'e is not posseeble : though to say such does destroy my 'art ! "

And in view of this very explicit and very reasonable statement of his inability to act in the premises, quite the most notable feature of the wedding was Jaune d'Antimoine's brilliant discharge of the functions of best man, in a resplendent suit of clothes that made him the delight of Rose Carthame's eyes, and the admiration of all Greenwich for many, many days.

The wedding was a quiet affair in St. Luke's Church, with a lunch in old Madder's studio afterward—at which Uncle Mangan made a speech that was all the better because he choked a good deal over it, and had to wipe his eyes with a big silk handkerchief two or three times, and that came to an end by his fairly breaking down. And Jaune d'Antimoine, clad in his garments of truly Oriental magnificence, gave the health of the bridemaids—Rose Carthame and Verona—in a most wonderful mingling of French and English ; and Cremnitz White, not trusting himself in English at all, made a most eloquent and feeling speech in German, that nobody understood, and that was applauded rapturously ; and old Madder made a speech in which he got miles away from the wedding into a disquisition upon the nobility and lastingness of Art that was edifying to listen to ; and little Sap Green was the only person present who was thoroughly and persistently melancholy from first to last. There was good reason for Sap Green's melancholy. It was bad enough for him to lose Rose, but it was worse still to know that a blight had fallen upon his hopes of fame : for his " Yorktown " never went to Philadelphia, and his certainty of a medal was dashed utterly, for the sorry reason that he had been unable to pay for the eight-by-ten-foot frame !

JAUNE D'ANTIMOINE.

DOWN Greenwich way—that is to say, about in the heart of the city of New York—in a room with a glaring south light that made even the thought of painting in it send shivers all over you, Jaune d'Antimoine lived and labored in the service of Art.

By all odds, it was the very worst room in the whole building ; and that was precisely the reason why Jaune d'Antimoine had chosen it, for the rent was next to nothing : he would have preferred a room that rented for even less. It certainly was a forlorn-looking place. There was no furniture in it worth speaking of; it was cheerless, desolate. A lot of studies of animals were stuck against the walls, and a couple of finished pictures—a lioness with her cubs, and a span of stunning draught-horses—stood in one corner, frameless. There was good work in the studies, and the pictures really were capital—a fact that Jaune himself recognized, and that made him feel all the more dismal because they so persistently remained unsold. Indeed, this animal-painter was having a pretty hard time of it, and as he sat there day after day in the shocking light, doing honest work and getting no return for it, he could not help growing desperately blue.

But to-day Jaune d'Antimoine was not blue, for of a sudden he had come to be stayed by a lofty purpose and upheld by a high resolve : and his purpose and resolve were that within one month's time he would gain for himself a new suit of clothes ! There were several excellent reasons which together served to fortify him in his exalted resolution. The most careless observer could not fail to perceive that the clothes which he wore—and which were incomparably superior to certain others which he possessed but did not wear—were sadly shabby ;

and Vandyke Brown had asked him to be
best man at his wedding ; and further—and
this was the strongest reason of all—Jaune
d'Antimoine longed, from the very depths of
his soul, to make himself pleasing in the eyes
of Rose Carthame.

How she managed it none but herself
knew; but this charming young person,
although the daughter of a widowly exile of
France who made an uncertain living by
letting lodgings in the region between south
and west of Washington Square, always
managed to dress herself delightfully. It is
true that feminine analysis might reveal the
fact that the materials of which her gowns
were made were of the cheapest product of
the loom ; yet was feminine envy aroused—
yea, even in the dignified portion of Fifth
Avenue that lies not south but north of
Washington Square — by the undeniable
style of these same gowns, and by their
charming accord with the stylish gait and air
of the trig little body who wore them.
Therefore it was that when Monsieur Jaune

graciously was permitted to accompany Mademoiselle Rose in her jaunts into the grand quarter of the town, the propriety of her garments and the impropriety of his own brought a sense of desolation upon his spirit and a great heaviness upon his loyal heart.

For Jaune loved Rose absolutely to distraction. To say that he would have laid his coat in the mud for her to walk over does not—the condition of the coat being remembered—imply a very superior sort of devotion. He would have done more than this: he would have laid himself in the mud, and most gladly, that he might have preserved from contamination her single pair of nice shoes. Even a cool and unprejudiced person, being permitted to see these shoes—and he certainly would have been, for Rose made anything but a mystery of them—would have declared that such gallant sacrifice was well bestowed.

The ardor of Jaune's passion was increased—as has been common in love matters ever since the world began—by the knowledge that he had a rival; and this rival was a most dangerous rival, being none other than Madame Carthame's second-story-front lodger, the Count Siccatif de Courtray. Simply to be the second-story-front lodger carries with it a most notable distinction in a lodging-house; but to be that and a count too was a combination of splendors that placed Jaune's rival on a social pinnacle and kept him there. Not that counts are rare in the region between west and south of Washington Square; on the contrary, they are rather astonishingly plentiful. But the sort of count who is very rare indeed there is the count who pays his way as he goes along. Now, in the matter of payments, at least so far as Madame Carthame was concerned, the Count Siccatif de Courtray was exemplary.

That there was something of a mystery about this nobleman was undeniable. Among other things, he had stated that he was a relative of the Siccatifs of Harlem—the old family established here in New Amsterdam in the early days of the Dutch Colony. Persons disposed to comment invidiously upon this asserted relationship, and such there were, did not fail to draw attention to the fact that the Harlem Siccatifs, without exception, were fair, while the Count Siccatif de Courtray was strikingly dark; and to the further fact that, if the distinguished American family really was akin to the Count, its several members were most harmoniously agreed to give him the cold shoulder. With these malicious whisperings, however, Madame Carthame did not concern herself. She was content, more than content, to take the Count as he was, and at his own valuation. That he was a proscribed Bonapartist, as he declared himself to be, seemed to her a reasonable and entirely credible statement ; and it certainly had the effect of creating about him a halo of romance. Though not proscribed, Madame Carthame herself was a Bonapartist, and a most ardent one ; a fact, it may be observed, concerning which the Count assured

himself prior to the avowal of his own politi-
cal convictions.   When, on the 20th of
April, he came home wearing a cluster of
violets in his button-hole, and bearing also a
bunch of these Imperial flowers for Madame
Carthame, and with the presentation confessed his own imperialistic faith and touched
gloomily upon the sorry reward that it had
brought him—when this event occurred,
Madame Carthame's kindly feelings toward
her second-floor lodger were resolved into
an abiding faith and high esteem.   It was
upon this auspicious day that the conviction
took firm root in her mind that the Count
Siccatif de Courtray was the heaven-sent
husband for her daughter Rose.

That Rose approved this ambitious matrimonial project of her mother's was a matter
open to doubt ; at least her conduct was such
that two diametrically opposite views were
entertained in regard to her intentions.   On
the one hand, Madame Carthame and the
Count Siccatif de Courtray believed that she
had made up her mind to live in her mother's

own second-story front and be a countess. On the other hand, Jaune d'Antimoine, whose wish, perhaps, was father to his thought, believed that she would not do anything of the sort. Jaune gladly would have believed, also, that she cherished matrimonial intentions in quite a different, namely, an artistic, direction ; but he was a modest young fellow, and suffered his hopes to be greatly diluted by his fears. And, in truth, the conduct of Rose was so perplexing, at times so atrociously exasperating, that a person much more deeply versed in women's ways than this young painter was, very well might have been puzzled hopelessly ; for if ever a born flirt came out of France, that flirt was Rose Carthame.

Of one thing, however, Jaune was convinced : that unless something of a positive nature was done, and done speedily, for the improvement of his outward man, his chance of success would be gone forever. Already, Madame Carthame eyed his seedy garments askance ; already, for Rose had admitted the

truth of his suspicions in this dismal direction, Madame Carthame had instituted most
unfavorable comparisons between his own
chronic shabbiness and the no less chronic
splendor of the Count Siccatif de Courtray.
Therefore, it came to pass—out of his abstract need for presentable habiliments, out
of his desire to appear in creditable form at
Vandyke Brown's wedding, and, more than
all else, out of his love for Rose—that Jaune
d'Antimoine registered a mighty oath before
high heaven that within a month's time a
new suit of clothes should be his !

Yet the chances are that he would hav.
gone down Christopher Street to the North
River, and still further down, even into a
watery grave—as he very frequently thought
of doing during this melancholy period of
his existence—had not his fortunes suddenly
been irradiated by the birth in his mind of a
happy thought. It came to him in this wise :
He was standing drearily in front of a ready-
made clothing store on Broadway, sadly
contemplating a wooden figure clad in pre-

cisely the morning suit for which his soul panted, when suddenly something gave him a whack in the back. Turning sharply, and making use of an exclamation not to be found in the French dictionaries compiled for the use of young ladies' boarding-schools, he perceived a wooden frame-work, from the lower end of which protruded the legs of a man. From a cleft in the upper portion of the frame-work came the apologetic utterance, " Didn't mean ter hit yer, boss," and then the structure moved slowly away through the throng. Over its four sides, he observed, were blazoned announcements of the excellences of the garments manufactured by the very clothing establishment in front of which he stood.

The thought came idly into his mind that this method of advertising was clumsy, and not especially effective ; followed by the further thought that a much better plan would be to set agoing upon the streets a really gentlemanly-looking man, clad in the best garments that the tailoring people manufactured—while a handsome sign upon the man's back, or a silken banner proudly borne aloft, should tell where the clothes were made, and how, for two weeks only, clothes equally excellent could be bought there at a tremendous sacrifice. And then came into his mind the great thought of his life: he would disguise himself by changing his blonde hair and beard to gray, and by wearing dark eye-glasses, and thus disguised he would be that man! Detection he believed to be impossible, for merely dressing himself in respectable clothes almost would suffice to prevent his recognition by even the nearest of his friends. With that prompt decision which is the sure sign of genius backed by force of character, he paused no longer to consider. He acted. With a firm step he entered the clothing establishment; with dignity demanded a personal interview with its roprietor; with eloquence presented to that personage his scheme.

"You will understand, sare," he said, in conclusion, "that these clothes such as yours see themselves in the best way when they are carried by a man very well made, and who 'as the air *comme il faut.* I 'ave not the custom to say that I am justly that man. But now we talk of *affaires.* Look at me and see!" And so speaking, he drew himself up his full six feet, and turned slowly around. There could not be any question about it : a handsomer, a more distinguished-looking man was not to be found in all New York. With the added dignity of age, his look of distinction would be but increased.

The great head of the great tailoring establishment was visibly affected. Original devices in advertising had been the making of him. He perceived that the device now suggested to him was superior to anything that his own genius had struck out. "It's a pretty good plan," he said, meditatively. "What do you want for carrying it out?"

"For you to serve two weeks, I ask but the clothes I go to wear."

For a moment the tailor paused. In that moment the destinies of Jaune d'Antimoine, of Rose Carthame, of the Count Siccatif de Courtray, hung in the balance. It was life or death. Jaune felt his heart beating like a trip-hammer. There was upon him a feeling of suffocation. The silence seemed interminable ; and the longer it lasted, the more did he feel that his chances of success were oozing away, that the crisis of his life was going against him. Darkness, the darkness of desolate despair, settled down upon his soul. Mechanically he felt in his waistcoat pocket for a five-cent piece that he believed to be there—for the stillness, the restful oblivion of the North River were in his mind. His fingers clutched the coin convulsively, thankfully. At least he would not be compelled to walk down Christopher Street to his death : he could pay his way to eternity in the one-horse car. Yet even while the blackness of shattered hope seemed to be closing him in irrevocably, the glad light came again. As the voice of an angel, sounded the voice of the tailor ; and the words which the tailor spake were these :

"Young man, it's a bargain!"

But the tailor, upon whom Heaven had bestowed shrewdness to an extraordinary degree, perceived in the plan proposed to him higher, more artistic possibilities than had been perceived in it by its inventor. There was a dramatic instinct, an appreciation of surprise, of climax, in this man's mind that he proceeded to apply to the existing situation. With a wave of his hand he banished the suggested sign on the walking-advertiser's back, and the suggested silken banner. His plan at once was simpler and more profound. Dressed in the highest style of art, Jaune was to walk Broadway daily between the hours of 11 A.M. and 2 P.M. He was to walk slowly; he was to look searchingly in the faces of all young women of about the age of twenty years; he was to wear, over and above his garments of price, an air of confirmed melancholy. That was all.

"But of the advertisement? 'Ow ——"

"Now, never you mind about the advertisement, young man. Where that is going to come in is my business. But you can just bet your bottom dollar that I don't intend to lose any money on you. All that you have to do is just what I've told you ; and to be well dressed, and walk up and down Broadway for three hours every day, and look in all the girls' faces, don't strike me as being the hardest work that you might be set at. Now come along and be measured, and day after to-morrow you shall begin."

As Jaune walked slowly homeward to his dismal studio, he meditated deeply upon the adventure before him. He did not fancy it at all ; but it was the means to an end, and he was braced morally to go through with it without flinching. For the chance of winning Rose he would have stormed a battery single-handed ; and not a bit more of moral courage would have been needed for such desperate work than was needed for the execution of the bloodless but soul-trying project that he had in hand. For the life and spirit of him, though, he could not see how the tailor was to get any good out of this magnificent masquerading.

IN one of the evening papers, about a week later, there appeared a half-column romance that quite took Jaune d'Antimoine's breath away. It began with a reference to the distinguished elderly gentleman who, during the past week, had been seen daily upon Broadway about the hour of noon; who gazed with such intense though respectful curiosity into every young woman's face; who, in the gay crowd, was conspicuous not less by the elegance of his dress than by his air of profound melancholy. Then briefly, but precisely, the sorrowful story of the Marquis de—— ("out of consideration for the nobleman's feelings," the name was withheld) was told: how, the son of a peer of France, he had married, while yet a minor, against the wishes of his stern father; how his young wife and infant daughter had been spirited away by the stern father's orders; how on his death-bed the father had confessed his evil deed to his son, and had told that mother and child had been banished to America, where the mother speedily had died of grief, and where the child, though in ignorance of her noble origin, had been adopted by an enormously rich American, about whom nothing more was known than the fact that he lived in New York. The Marquis, the article stated, now was engaged in searching for his long-lost daughter, and among other means to the desired end had hit upon this—of walking New York's chief thoroughfare in the faith that should he see his child his paternal instinct would reveal to him her identity.

"I calculate that this will rather whoop up public interest in our performance," said the tailor, cheerfully, the next day, as he handed the newspaper containing the pleasing fiction to Jaune. "That's my idea, for a starter. I've got the whole story ready to come out in sections—paid a literary feller twenty dollars to get it up for me. And you be careful to-day when you are interviewed" (Jaune shuddered) "to keep the story up—or" (for Jaune was beginning a remonstrance) "you can keep out of it altogether, if you'd rather. Say you must refuse to talk upon so delicate a subject, or something of that sort. Yes, that's your card. It'll make the mystery greater, you know—and I'll see that the public gets the facts, all the same."

The tailor chuckled, and Jaune was unutterably wretched. He was on the point of throwing up his contract. He opened his mouth to speak the decisive words—and shut it again as the thought came into his mind that his misery must be borne, and borne gallantly, because it was all for the love of Rose.

That day there was no affectation in his air of melancholy. He was profoundly miserable. Faithful to his contract, he looked searchingly upon the many young women of twenty years whom he met; and such of them as were possessors of tender hearts grew very sorrowful at sight of the obvious woe by which he was oppressed. His woe, indeed, was keen, for the newspaper article had had its destined effect, and he was a marked man. People turned to look at him as people had not turned before; it was evident that he was a subject of conversation. Several times he caught broken sentences which he recognized as portions of his supposititious biography. His crowning torture was the assault of the newspaper reporters. They were suave, they were surly, they were insinuatingly sympathetic, they were aggressively peremptory—but all alike were determined to wring from him to the uttermost the details of the sorrow that he never had suffered, of the life that he never had lived. It was a confusing sort of an experience. He began to wonder, at last, whether or not it were possible that he could be somebody else without knowing it; and if it were, in whom, precisely, his identity was vested. Being but a simple-minded young fellow, with no taste whatever for metaphysics, this line of thought was upsetting.

While involved in these perplexing doubts and the crowd at the Fifth Avenue crossing, he was so careless as to step upon the heel of a lady in front of him. And when the lady turned, half angrily, half to receive his profuse apologies, he beheld Mademoiselle Carthame. The face of this young person wore an expression made up of not less than three conflicting emotions : of resentment of the assault upon the heel of her one pair of good shoes, of friendly recognition of the familiar voice, of blank surprise upon perceiving that this voice came from the lips of a total stranger. She looked searchingly upon the smoked glasses, obviously trying to pry into the secret of the hidden eyes. Jaune's blood rushed up into his face, and he realized that detection was imminent. Mercifully, at that moment the crowd opened, and with a bow that hid his face behind his hat he made good his retreat. During the remaining half hour of his walk, he thought no more of metaphysics. The horrid danger of physical discovery from which he had escaped so narrowly filled him with a shuddering alarm. Nor could he banish from his mind the harrowing thought that perhaps, for all his gray hair and painted wrinkles and fine clothes, Rose in truth had recognized him.

That night an irresistible attraction drew him to the Carthame abode. In the little parlor he found the severe Madame Carthame, her adorable daughter, and the offensive Count Siccatif de Courtray. Greatly to his relief, his reception was in the usual form : Madame Carthame conducted herself after the fashion of a well-bred iceberg ; Rose endeavored to mitigate the severity of her parent's demeanor by her own affability ; the Count, as much as possible, ignored his presence. Jaune could not repress a sigh of relief. She had not recognized him.

But his evening was one of trial. With much vivacity, Rose entertained the little company with an account of her romantic adventure with the French nobleman who had come to America in quest of his lost daughter; for she had read the newspaper story, and had identified its hero with the assailant of her heel. She dwelt with enthusiasm upon the distinguished appearance of the unhappy foreigner; she ventured the suggestion, promptly and sternly checked by her mamma, that she herself might be the lost child; she grew plaintive, and expressed a burning desire to comfort this stricken parent with a daughter's love; and, worst of all, she sat silent, with a far-away look in her charming eyes, and obviously suffered her thoughts to go astray after this handsome Marquis in a fashion that made even the Count Siccatif de Courtray fidget, and that filled the soul of Jaune d'Antimoine with a consuming jealousy—not the less consuming because of the absurd fact that it was jealousy of himself! As he walked home that night through the devious ways of Greenwich to his dismal studio, he seriously entertained the wish that he never had been born.

The next day all the morning papers contained elaborate "interviews" with the Marquis : for each of the several reporters who had been put on the case, believing that he alone had failed to get the facts, and being upheld by a lofty determination that no other reporter should "get a beat on him," had evolved from his own inner consciousness the story that Jaune, for the best of reasons, had refused to tell. The stories thus told, being based upon the original fiction, bore a family resemblance to each other ; and as all of them were interesting, they stimulated popular curiosity in regard to their hero to a very high pitch. As the result of them, Jaune found himself the most conspicuous man in New York. During the three hours of his walk he was the centre of an interested crowd. Several benevolent persons stopped him to tell him of fatherless young women with whom they were acquainted, and to urge upon him the probability that each of these young women was his long-lost child. The representatives of a dozen detective bureaus introduced themselves to him, and made offer of their professional services; a messenger from the chief of police handed him a polite note tendering the services of the department and inviting him to a conference. It was maddening.

But worst of all were his meetings with Rose. As these multiplied, the conviction became irresistible that they were not the result of chance; indeed, her manner made doubt upon this head impossible. At first she gave him only a passing glance, then a glance somewhat longer, then a look of kindly interest, then a long look of sympathy; and at last she bestowed upon him a gentle, almost affectionate, smile that expressed, as plainly as a smile could express, her sorrow for his misery and her readiness to comfort him. In a word, Rose Carthame's conduct simply was outrageous!

The jealous anger which had inflamed Jaune's breast the night before swelled and expanded into a raging passion. He longed to engage in mortal combat this stranger who was alienating the affection that should be his. The element of absurdity in the situation no longer was apparent to him. In truth, as he reasoned, the situation was not absurd. To all intents and purposes he was two people : and it was the other one of him, not himself at all, who was winning Rose's interest, perhaps her love. For a moment the thought crossed his mind that he would adjust the difficulty in his own favor by remaining this other person always. But the hard truth confronted him that every time he washed his face he would cease to be the elderly Marquis, with the harder truth that the fabulous wealth with which, as the Marquis, the newspapers had endowed him was too entirely fabulous to serve as a basis for substantial life. And being thus cut off from hope, he fell back upon jealous hatred of himself.

That night the evening paper in which the first mention of the mysterious French nobleman had been made, contained an article cleverly contrived to give point to the

mystery in its commercial aspect. The fact
had been observed, the article declared, that
the nobleman's promenade began and ended
at a prominent clothing establishment on
Broadway; and then followed, in the guise
of a contribution toward the clearing up of
the mystery, an interview with the proprietor
of the establishment in question. However,
the interview left the mystery just where it
found it, for all that the tailor told was that
the Marquis had bought several suits of
clothes from him; that he had shown himself to be an exceptionally critical person in
the matter of his wearing apparel; that he
had expressed repeatedly his entire satisfaction with his purchases. In another portion
of the paper was a glaring advertisement, in
which the clothing man set forth, in an ani-
mated fashion, the cheapness and desirability
of "The Marquis Suit"—a suit that "might
be seen to advantage on the person of the
afflicted French nobleman now in our midst,
who had honored it with his approval, and
in whose honor it had been named." Upon

reading the newspaper narrative and its advertisement pendent, Jaune groaned aloud. He was oppressed by a horror of discovery, and here, as it seemed to him in his morbidly nervous condition, was a clew to his duplex identity sufficiently obvious to be apparent even to a detective.

THE Count Siccatif de Courtray, as has been intimated, went so far as to fidget while listening to Mademoiselle Carthame's vivacious description of her encounter with the handsome Marquis. Being regaled during the ensuing evening with a very similar narrative—a materially modified version of the events which had aroused in so lively a manner the passion of jealousy in the breast of Jaune d'Antimoine—the Count ceased merely to fidget, and became the prey to a serious anxiety. He determined that the next day, quite unobtrusively, he would observe Mademoiselle Carthame in her relations with this unknown but dangerously fascinating nobleman; and also that he would give some attention to the nobleman himself. This secondary purpose was strengthened the next morning, while the Count was engaged with his coffee and newspaper, by his finding in the "Courrier des États-Unis" a translation of the paragraph stating the curious fact that the daily walk of the Marquis began and ended at the Broadway tailor-shop.

Having finished his breakfast, the Count leisurely betook himself to Broadway. As he slowly strolled eastward, he observed on the other side of the street Jaune d'Antimoine, in his desperately shabby raiment, hurriedly walking eastward also. The Count murmured a brief panegyric upon M. d'Antimoine, in which the words "cet animal" alone were distinguishable. They were near Broadway at this moment, and to the Count's surprise M. d'Antimoine entered the clothing establishment from which the Marquis departed upon his daily walk. Could it be possible, he thought, that fortune had smiled upon the young artist, and that he was about to purchase a new suit of clothes? The

Count entertained the charitable hope that such could not be the case.

It was the Count's purpose, in order that he might follow also the movements of Mademoiselle Carthame, to follow the Marquis from the beginning to the end of his promenade. He set himself, therefore, to watching closely for the appearance of the grief-stricken foreigner, moving carelessly the while from one shop-window to another that commanded a view of the field. At the end of half an hour, when the Count was beginning to think that the object of his solicitude was a myth, out from the broad portal of the clothing establishment came the Marquis in all his glory—more glorious, in truth, than Solomon, and more melancholy than the melancholy Jaques. And yet for an instant the Count Siccatif de Courtray was possessed by the absurd fancy that this stately personage was Jaune d'Antimoine ! Truly, here was the same tall, handsome figure, the same easy, elegant carriage, the same cut of hair and beard. But the resemblance went no further, for beard and hair were gray almost to whiteness, the face was pale and old, and the clothes, so far from being desperately seedy, were more resplendent even than the Count's own. No, the thought was incredible, preposterous, and yet the Count could not discharge it from his mind. He stamped his foot savagely; this mystery was becoming more interesting than pleasing.

In the crowd that the Marquis drew in his wake, as he slowly, sadly sauntered up Broadway, the Count had no difficulty in following him unobserved. The situation was that of the previous day, only it was intensified, and therefore, to its hero, the more horrible. The benevolent people with stray fatherless young women to dispose of were out in greater force; the detectives were more aggressive; the newspaper people were more persistent; the general public was more keenly interested in the whole performance. And Rose—most dreadful of all—was more outrageous than ever! The

Count grew almost green with rage during the three hours that he was a witness of this young woman's scandalous conduct. A dozen times she met the Marquis in the course of his walk, and each time that she met him she greeted him with a yet more tender smile. A curious fact that at first surprised, then puzzled, then comforted the Count was the very obvious annoyance which these flattering attentions caused their recipient. Evidently, he persistently endeavored to evade the meetings which Rose as persistently and more successfully endeavored to force upon him. Within the scope of M. de Courtray's comprehension only one reason seemed to be sufficient to explain the determination on the part of the Marquis to resist the advances of a singularly attractive young woman, whose good disposition toward him was so conspicuously, though so irregularly, manifested: a fear of recognition. And this reason adjusted itself in a striking manner to the queer notion that had come into his mind that the Marquis was an ideal creation, whose reality was Jaune d'Antimoine. The thought was absurd, irrational, but it grew stronger and stronger within him—and became an assured conviction when, shortly after the promenade of the Marquis had ended, Jaune came forth from the clothing-store in his normal condition of shabbiness and youth. The Count was not in all respects a praiseworthy person, but among his vices was not that of stupidity. Without any very tremendous mental effort he grasped the fact that his rival had sold himself into bondage as a walking advertisement, and, knowing this, a righteous exultation filled his soul. Jaune's destiny, so far as Mademoiselle Carthame was concerned, he felt was in his power: and he was perplexed by no nice doubts as to the purpose to which the power that he had gained should be applied.

Untroubled by the knowledge that his secret was discovered, Jaune entered upon the last day of his martyrdom. It was the most agonizing day of all. The benevolent

persons, the reporters, the detectives, the
crowd surging about him, drove him almost
to madness. He walked as one dazed. And
above and over all he was possessed by a
frenzy of jealousy that came of the offen-
sively friendly smiles which Rose bestowed
upon him as she forced meetings upon him
again and again. It was with difficulty that
he restrained himself from laying violent
hands upon this bogus Marquis who falsely
and infamously had beguiled away from him
the love for which he gladly would have
given his life. Only the blood of his despic-
able rival, he felt, would satisfy him. He
longed to find himself with a sword in his
hand on a bit of smooth turf, and the villain-
ous Marquis over against him, ready to be
run through. The thought was so delightful, so animating, that involuntarily he made
a lunge—and had to apologize confusedly to
the elderly gentleman whom he had poked in
the back with his umbrella.

At last the three hours of torture, the last
of his two weeks of hateful servitude, came

to an end. Pale beneath his false paleness, haggard beyond his false haggardness of age, he entered the clothing-store and once more was himself. With a gladness unspeakable he washed off his wrinkles and washed out the gray from his hair and beard; with a sense of infinite satisfaction that, a fortnight earlier, he would not have believed possible, he resumed his shabby old clothes. Had he chosen to do so, he might have walked away in the new and magnificent apparel which he now fairly had earned; but just at present his loathing for these fine garments was beyond all words.

The tailor fain would have had the masquerade continue longer, for, as he frankly stated, "The Marquis Suit" was having a tremendous sale. But Jaune was deaf not only to the tailor's blandishments, but to his offers of substantial cash. "Not for the millions would I be in this part of the Marquis for one day yet more," he said firmly. And he added, "I trust to you in honor, sare, that not never shall my name be spoken in this affair."

"Couldn't speak it if I wanted to, my dear boy. It's a mystery to me how you're able to say it yourself! Well, I'd like you to run the ' Marquis ' for another week; but if you won't, you won't, I suppose, so there's an end of it. I'm sorry you haven't enjoyed it. I have. It's been as good a thing as I ever got hold of. Now give me your address and I'll have your clothes sent to you. Don't you want some more ? I don't mind letting you have a regular outfit if you want it. One good turn, you know— and you've done me a good turn, and that's a fact."

But Jaune declined this liberal offer, and declined also to leave his address, which would have involved a revelation of his name. It was a comfort to him to know that his name was safe—a great comfort. So the garments of the forever-departed Marquis were but up in a big bundle, and Jaune journeyed homeward to his studio in Greenwich —bearing his sheaves with him—in a Bleecker Street car.

"WELL, you are a cheeky beggar, d'Antimoine," said Vandyke Brown, cheerfully, the next morning, as he came into Jaune's studio with a newspaper in his hand. "So you are the Marquis who has been setting the town wild for the last week, eh? And who did you bet with? And what started you in such a crazy performance, anyway? Tell me all about it. It's as funny—Good heavens! d'Antimoine, what's the matter? Are you ill?" For Jaune had grown deathly pale and was gasping.

"I do not know of what it is that you talk," he answered, with a great effort.

"Oh, come now, that's too thin, you know. Why, here's a whole column about it, telling how you made a bet with somebody that you could set all the town to talking about you, and yet do it all in such a clever disguise that nobody would know who you really were, not even your most intimate friends. And I should say that you had won handsomely. Why, I've seen you on Broadway a dozen times myself this last week, and I never had the remotest suspicion that the Marquis was you. I must say, though," continued Brown, reflectively, and looking closely at Jaune, " that it was stupid of me. I did think that you had a familiar sort of look; and once, I remember, it did occur to me that you looked astonishingly like your-self. It—it was the clothes, you see, that threw me out. Where ever did you get such a stunning rig? I don't believe that I'd have known you dressed like that, even if you hadn't been gray and wrinkled. But tell me all about it, old man. It must have been jolly fun !"

" Fun ! " groaned Jaune ; " it was the de-spair ! " And then, his heart being very full and his longing for sympathy overpowering, Jaune told Brown the whole story. " But what is this of one bet, my dear Van," he concluded, " I do not of the least know."

" Well, here it all is in the paper, anyway. Calls you ' a distinguished animal-painter,' and alludes to your ' strikingly vigorous " Lioness and Cubs " and powerful " Dray

Horses" at the last spring exhibition of the
Society of American Artists.' Must be somebody who knows you, you see, and somebody who means well by you, too. There's
nothing at all about your being an advertisement; indeed, there's nothing in the story
but a good joke, of which you are the hero.
It's an eccentric sort of heroism, to be sure;
but then, for some unknown reason, people
never seem to believe that artists are rational
human beings, so your eccentricity will do
you no harm. And it's no end of an advertisement for you. Whoever wrote it meant
well by you. And, by Jove! I know who
it is! It's little Conté Crayon. He's a
good-hearted little beggar, and he likes you
ever so much, for I've heard him say so;
but how he ever got hold of the story, and
especially of such a jolly version of it, I don't
see."

At this moment, by a pleasing coincidence,
Conté Crayon himself appeared with the desired explanation. "You see," he said,
"that beast of a Siccatif de Courtray hunted

me up yesterday and told me the yarn about you and the slop-shop man. · He wanted me to write it up and publish it, 'as a joke,' he said; but it was clear enough that he was in ugly earnest about it. And so, you see, I had to rush it into print in the way I chose to tell it—which won't do you a bit of harm, d'Antimoine—in order to head him off. The blackguard meant to get you into a mess, and if I'd hung fire he'd have told somebody else about it, and had the real story published. Of course, you know, there's nothing in the real story that you need be ashamed of; but if it had been told, you certainly would have been laughed at, and nasty people would have said nasty things about it. And as there wasn't any time to lose, I had to print it first and then come here and explain matters afterward. And what I've got to say is this : Just you cheek it out and say that it *was* a bet, and that you won it ! Brown and I will back you up in it, and so will the slop-shop man. I've been to see him this morning, and he is so pleased with the way that 'The Marquis Suit' is selling, and with the extra free ad-/ertisement that he has got out of my article, that he's promised to adopt the bet version in his advertisement in all the papers. He is going to advertise that The Marquis Suit is so called because everybody who wears it looks like a marquis—just as you did. This cuts the ground right from under the Count's feet, you see; for nobody'd believe him on his oath if they could help it.

"And now I must clear out. I've got a race at Jerome Park at two o'clock. It's all right, d'Antimoine; I assure you it's all right—but I should advise you to punch the Count's head, all the same."

Vandyke Brown thought that it was all right, too, as he talked the matter over with Jaune after little Conté Crayon had gone. But Jaune refused to be comforted. So far as the public was concerned he admitted that Conté Crayon's story had saved him, but he was oppressed by a great dread of what might be the effect of the truth upon Rose.

For Jaune d'Antimoine was too honest a gentleman even to think of deceiving his mistress. He must tell her the whole story, without reserve, and as she approved or disapproved of what he had done must his hopes of happiness live or die.

"Better have it out with her to-day, and be done with it," counselled Brown.

"Ah! it is well for you to speak of a 'urry, my good Van; but it is not you who go to execute your life. No, I 'ave not the force to go to-day. To-day I go to make a long walk. Then this night I sleep well. To-morrow, in the morning, do I go to affront my destiny." And from this resolution Jaune was not to be moved.

Yet it was an unfortunate resolution, for it gave the Count Siccatif de Courtray time and opportunity for a flank movement. In the Count's breast rage and astonishment contended for the mastery as he contemplated the curious miscarriage of his newspaper assault. He had chosen this line of attack partly because his modesty counselled him to keep his own personality in the background, partly because the wider the publicity of his rival's disgrace the more complete would that disgrace be. But as his newspaper ally had failed him, he took the campaign into his own hands ; that is to say, he hurried to tell the true story, and a good deal more than the true story, to Rose and Madame Carthame.

Concerning its effect upon Rose, he was in doubt; but its effect upon Madame Carthame was all that he could desire. This severe person instantly took the cue that the Count dexterously gave her by affecting to palliate Jaune's erratic conduct. He urged that, inasmuch as M. d'Antimoine was a conspicuous failure as an artist, for him to engage himself to a tailor as a walking advertisement, so far from being a disgrace to him, was greatly to his credit. And Madame Carthame promptly and vehemently asserted that it wasn't. She refused to regard what he had done in any other light than that of a crime. She declared that never again should his offensive form darken her door. Solemnly she forbade Rose from recognizing him when in the future they should chance to meet. And then she abated her severity to the extent of thanking the Count with tears in her eyes for the service that he had done her in tearing off this viper's disguise. Naturally, the Count was charmed by Madame Carthame's energetic indignation. He perceived that his unselfish investigations of the actions of Monsieur Jaune were bearing excellent fruit. Already, as he believed, the way toward his own happiness was smooth and clear. As the Count retired from this successful conference, he laughed softly to himself: nor did he pause in his unobtrusive mirth to reflect that those laugh best who laugh last.

And thus it came to pass that when Jaune, refreshed by sound slumber and a little cheered by hope, presented himself the next morning at Madame Carthame's gates, fate decreed that Rose herself should open the gates to him—in response to his ring—and in her own proper person should tell him that she was not at home. In explanation of this obviously inexact statement she announced to him her mother's stern decree. Being but a giddy young person, however, and one somewhat lacking in fit reverence of maternal authority, she added, on her own account, that in half an hour or so she was going up Fourth Street to the Gansevoort market, and that Fourth Street was a public thoroughfare, upon which M. d'Antimoine also had a perfect right to walk.

In the course of this walk, while Jaune gallantly carried the market-basket, the story that Rose already had heard from the Count Siccatif de Courtray was told again—but told with a very different coloring. For Mademoiselle Carthame clearly perceived how great the sacrifice had been that Jaune had made for her sake, and how bravely, because it was for her sake, it had been made. There was real pathos in his voice; once or twice he nearly broke down. Possibly it was because she did not wish him to

see her eyes that she manifested so marked
an interest in the shop windows as they
walked along.

"And so that adorable Marquis was
unreal?" queried Mademoiselle Carthame
sadly, and somewhat irrelevantly, when
Jaune had told her all.

"He was not adorable. He was a dis-
gusting beast!" replied M. d'Antimoine savagely.

"I—I loved him!" answered Rose, turning upon Jaune, at last, her black eyes.
They did not sparkle, as was their wont, but
they were wonderfully lustrous and soft.

Jaune looked down into the market-basket
and groaned.

"And—and I love him still. I think, I—
I hope, that he will live always in my heart."

The voice of Mademoiselle Carthame trembled, and her hand grasped very tightly the
bag of carrots that they had been unable to
make a place for in the basket: they were
coming back from the market now.

Jaune did not look up. For the life of

him he could not keep back a sob. It was bitter hard, he felt, that out of his love for Rose should come love's wreck ; and, harder yet that the rival who had stolen her from him should be himself ! Through the mist of his misery he seemed to hear Rose laughing softly. Could this be so ? Then, indeed, was the capstone set upon his grief !

" Jaune !"

He started, and so violently that a cabbage, with half a dozen potatoes after it, sprang out of the basket and rolled along the pavement at their feet. His bowed head rose with a jerk, and their eyes met full.   In hers there was a look half mocking, that as he gazed changed into tenderness ; into his, as he saw the change and perceived its meaning, there came a look of glad delight.

" As though you could deceive *me!* Why, of course, I knew you from the very first ! "

Then they collected the potatoes and the cabbage and walked slowly on, and great happiness was in their hearts.

The world was a brighter world for Jaune

d'Antimoine when he gave into Rose's hand the market-basket on her own door-step, and turned reluctantly away. But there still were clouds in it. Rose had admitted that two things were necessary before getting married could be thought of at all seriously: something must be done by which the nose of the Count Siccatif de Courtray would be disjointed; something must be done to assure Madame Carthame that M. d'Antimoine, in some fashion at least a little removed from semi-starvation, could maintain a wife. It was certain that until these things were accomplished Madame Carthame's lofty resolution to transform her daughter into a countess, and her stern disapprobation of Jaune as a social outcast, never would be overcome.

As events turned out, it was the second of these requirements that was fulfilled first.

MR. BADGER BRUSH was a very rich sporting man, whose tastes were horsey, but whose heart was in the right place. It was his delight to make or to back extraordinary wagers. Few New Yorkers have forgotten that very queer bet of his that resulted in putting high hats on all the Broadway telegraph poles. When Mr. Brush read the story of Jaune d'Antimoine's wager, therefore, he was greatly pleased with its originality; and when, later in the day, he fell in with little Conté Crayon at Jerome Park, he pressed that ingenious young newspaper man for additional particulars. And knowing the whereabouts of Mr. Badger Brush's heart, Conté Crayon did not hesitate to tell the whole story—winding up with the pointed suggestion that inasmuch as the hero of the story was an animal-painter of decided, though as yet unrecognized, ability, Mr. Brush could not do better than manifest his interest in a practical way by giving him an order. The sporting man rose to the suggestion with a commendable promptness and warmth.

"I don't care a blank if it wasn't a bet," he said, heartily. "That young man has pluck, and he deserves to be encouraged. I'll go down and see him to-morrow, and I'll order a portrait of Celeripes ; a life-size, thousand-dollar portrait, by Jove !   Celeripes deserves it, after the pot of money he brought me at Long Branch, and your friend deserves it too.   And I have some other horses that I want painted, and some dogs— he paints dogs, I suppose ?   And I know a lot of other fellows who ought to have their horses painted, and I'll start them along at him.   I'll give him all the painting he can handle in the next ten years.   For it *was* a bet, you see, after all.   Didn't he back his cleverness in disguise against the wits of the whole town ?   And didn't the slop-shop man put up the stakes ?   And didn't he just win in a canter ?   I should rather think he did ! Of course it was a bet, and a mighty good one at that.   Gad ! Crayon, it's the best thing that's been done in New York for years.   It's what I call first-class cheek.   I couldn't have done it better, sir, myself ! "

Thus it fell out that half an hour after

Jaune got back to his studio from that memorable walk to the Gansevoort market, he had the breath-taking-away felicity of booking a thousand-dollar order, and of receiving such obviously trustworthy assurances of many more orders that his wildest hopes of success in a moment were resolved into substantial realities. When he was alone again he certainly would have believed that he had been dreaming but for the fact that Mr. Badger Brush had insisted upon paying half the price of the picture down in advance; for whatever this good-hearted, horsey gentleman did, he did thoroughly well. The crisp notes, more than Jaune ever had seen together in all his life before—save once, when he took a dealer's cheque for ten dollars to a bank and looked through the wire screen while the bank man haughtily cashed it—lay on the table where Mr. Badger Brush had left them; and their blissful presence proved that his happiness was not a dream, but real.

From the corner into which, loathingly,

he had kicked it, he drew forth the bundle containing "The Marquis Suit." With a certain solemnity he resumed these garments of price in which he had suffered so much torture, and, being clad, boldly presented himself to Madame Carthame with a formal demand for her daughter's hand. And in view of the sudden and prodigious change that had come over M. d'Antimoine's fortunes, almost was Madame Carthame persuaded that the matrimonial plans which she had laid out for her daughter might be changed. Yet did she hesitate before announcing that their Median and Persian quality might be questioned : for the hope that Rose might be a countess lay very close to Madame Carthame's heart. However, her determination was shaken, which was a great point gained.

And presently—for Jaune's star was triumphantly in the ascendant—it was completely destroyed. The instrument of its destruction was Mr. Badger Brush's groom, Stumps.

Stumps was a talkative creature, and whenever he came down to Jaune's studio, as he very often did while the portrait of Celeripes was in progress, he had a good deal to say over and above the message that he brought, as to when the horse would be free for the next " sitting " in the paddock at Mr. Brush's country place where Jaune was painting him. And Jaune, who was one of the best-natured of mortals, usually suffered Stumps to talk away until he was tired.

" You might knock me down with a wisp of hay, you might, indeed, sir," said the groom one morning a fortnight after the picture had been begun—the day but one, in fact, before that set for Vandyke Brown's wedding. " Yes, sir," he continued, " with a wisp of hay, or even with a single straw ! Here I've been face to face with my own father's brother's son, and I've put out my hand to him, and he's turned away short and pretended as he didn't know me and went off ! And they tells me at his lodgin', for I follered him a-purpose to find him out, that he calls hisself a Frenchman, and says as how his name—which it is Stumps, and always has been—is Count Sikativ de Cortray!"

Jaune's palette and brushes fell to the floor with a crash. "Is it posseeble that you do tell me of the Comte Siccatif de Courtray? Are you then sure that you do not make one grand meestake? Is it 'im truly that you 'ave seen?"

"Him, sir? Wy, in course it's him. Haven't I knowed him ever since he wasn't higher'n a hoss's fetlock? Don't I tell you as me and him's fust cousins? Him? In course it's him—the gump!"

"Then, my good Stump, you will now tell me of this wonder all."

"It's not much there is to tell, sir, and wat there is isn't to his credit. His father was my father's brother. My father was in the hoss line out Saint John's Wood way— in Lunnon, you know, sir—and his father lived in our street and was a swell barber. Uncle'd married a French young 'ooman as was dressmakin' and had been a lady's maid;

it's along of his mother that he gets his
Frenchness, you see. He was an only son,
he was, and they made a lot of him—dressin'
him fine, and coddlin' him, and sendin' him
to school like anythink. Uncle was doin' a
big trade, you see, and makin' money fast.
Then, when he was a young fellow of twenty
or so, and after he'd served at barberin' with
his father for a couple of years, he took
service with young Lord Cadmium—as had
his ' cousin ' livin' in a willa down our way,
and came to uncle's to be barbered frequent. And wen Lord Cadmium went
sudden-like over to the Continent, wishin' to
give his ' cousin ' the slip, havin' got sick of
her, Stumps he went along. That's a matter of ten years ago, sir, and blessed if I've
laid eyes on him since until I seed him here
in New York to-day. Uncle died better'n
two year back, aunt havin' died fust, and he
left a tidy pot of money to Stumps ; and I
did hear that Stumps, who'd been barberin'
in Paris, had giv' up work when he got the
cash and had set up to be a gentleman, but

I didn't know as he'd set up to be a count too.   The like of this I never did see!"

" And you are, then, sure, you will swear, my good Stump, that this are the same man?"

" Swear, sir! I'll swear to it 'igh and low and all day long! But I must be goin', sir. You will please to remember that the hoss will be ready for you at ten o'clock to-morrow mornin', sharp."

Jaune rushed down to Vandyke Brown's studio for counsel as to whether he should go at once to the Count's lodgings and charge him with fraud to his face, or should make the charge first to Madame Carthame.   But Brown was out.   Nor was he in old Madder's studio, though about this time he was much more likely to be there than in his own. Old Madder said that Brown had taken Rose over to Brooklyn, to the Philharmonic, and he believed that they were going to dinner at Mr. Mangan Brown's afterward, and would not be in till late; and he seemed to be pretty grumpy about it.

Jaune fumed and fretted away what was left of the afternoon and a good part of the evening. At last Brown and Rose came home, and Brown, with a very bad grace, suffered himself to be led away from old Madder's threshold. To do him justice, though, when he had heard the story that Jaune had to tell, he was all eagerness. His advice was to make the attack instantly; and without more words they set off together, walking briskly through the chill air of the late October night.

As they were passing along Macdougal Street—midway between Bleecker and Houston, in front of the row of pretty houses with verandas all over their fronts—Jaune suddenly gripped Brown's arm and drew him quickly within one of the little front yards and into the shadow of the high iron steps.

" Look ! " he said.

On the other side of the street, in the light of the gas-lamp that stands in the centre of the block, was the Count himself. For the moment that he was beneath the gas-lamp they saw him clearly. His face was set in an expression of gloomy sternness; his rapid, resolute walk indicated a definite purpose; he carried a little bundle in his hand.

"What a villain he looks!" whispered Brown. "Upon my soul, I do believe that he is going to murder somebody!"

"Ah! the vile animal! We will pursue," answered Jaune, also in a whisper.

Giving the Count a start of a dozen house fronts, they stepped out from their retreat and followed him cautiously. He walked quickly up Macdougal Street until he came out on Washington Square. For a moment he paused—by Sam Wah's laundry—and then turned sharply to the left along Fourth Street. At a good pace he crossed Sixth Avenue, swung around the curve that Fourth Street makes before beginning its preposterous journey northward, went on past the three little balconied houses whose fronts are on Washington Place, and so came out upon the open space where Washington Place and

Barrow Street and Fourth Street all run into each other. It was hereabouts that Wouter Van Twiller had his tobacco farm a trifle less than two centuries ago.

The Count stopped, as though to get his bearings ; and while they waited for him to go on, Brown nudged Jaune to look at the delightfully picturesque frame house, set in a deep niche between two high brick houses, with the wooden stair elbowing up its outside to its third story. It came out wonderfully well in the moonlight, but Jaune was too much excited even to glance at it.

At the next group of corners—where Fourth Street crosses Grove and Christopher Streets at the point where they go sidling into each other along the slanting lines of the little park—the Count halted again. Evidently, the exceeding crookedness of Greenwich Village puzzled him—as well it might. Presently a Christopher-Street car came along and set him straight ; and thus guided, he started resolutely westward, as though heading for the river.

"Is it posseeble that he goes 'imself to drown?" suggested d'Antimoine.

"No such good luck," Brown answered shortly.

Coming out on what used to be called "the Strand"—West Street they call it now—the Count bore away from the lights of the Hoboken Ferry and from the guarded docks of the White Star and Anchor lines of steamers, skirted the fleet of oyster boats, and so came to the quiet pier at the foot of Perry Street, where the hay barges unload. This pier runs a long way out into the river, for it is a part of what was called Sapokamikke Point in Indian times. The Count stopped and looked cautiously around him, but his pursuers promptly crouched behind a dray and became invisible.

As he went out upon the pier, though, they were close upon his heels—walking noiselessly over the loose hay and keeping themselves hidden in the shadow of the barges and behind the piles of bales. At the very end of the pier he stopped. Jaune and Brown, hidden by a bale of hay, were within five feet of him. Their hearts were beating tremendously. There had been no tragical purpose in their minds when they started, but it certainly did look now as though they were in the thick of a tragedy. In the crisp October moonlight the Count's face shone deathly pale ; they could see the fingers of his right hand working convulsively; they could hear his labored breathing. Below him was the deep, black water, lapping and rippling as the swirl of the tide sucked it into the dark, slimy recesses among the piles. In its bosom was horrible death. The Count stepped out upon the very edge of the pier and gazed wofully down upon the swelling waters. His dismal purpose no longer admitted of doubt. Involuntarily the two followed him until they were close at his back. Little as they loved him, they could not suffer him thus despairingly to leave the world.

But instead of casting himself over the edge of the pier, the Count slowly raised the hand that held the bundle, with the obvious intention of throwing the bundle and whatever was the evil secret that it contained into the river's depths. Quick as thought, Brown had seized the upraised arm, and Jaune had settled upon the other arm with a grip like a vise.

"No you don't, my boy! Let's see what it is before it goes overboard. Hold fast, d'Antimoine!"

The Count struggled furiously, but hopelessly.

"It's no use. You may as well give in, Stumps!"

As Brown uttered this name the Count suddenly became limp. The little bundle that he had clutched tightly through the struggle dropped from his nerveless hand, and fell open as it struck the ground. And there, gleaming in the moonlight, a brace of razors, a stubby brush, a stout pair of shears, lay loosely in the folds of a barber's jacket!

And this was the sorry climax to the brilliant romance of the proscribed Bonapartist, the Count Siccatif de Courtray !

Jaune, who was a generous-hearted young fellow, was for setting free his crest-fallen rival at once, and so having done with him. Brown took a more statesmanlike view of the situation. "We will let him go after he has owned up to Madame Carthame what a fraud he is," he said. The Count winced when this sentence was pronounced, but he uttered no remonstrance. The shock of the discovery had completely demoralized him.

It was after midnight when they reached Madame Carthame's dwelling, and Rose herself, with her hair done up in curl papers, opened the door for them. When she recognized the three visitors and perceived that the Count was in custody, and at the same moment remembered her curl papers, on her face the gaze of astonishment and the blush of maidenly modesty contended for the right of way.

Madame Carthame fairly was in bed—as

was evident from the spirited conversation between herself and her vivacious daughter, that was perfectly audible through the folding doors which separated the little parlor from her bedroom. It was evident, also, that she was indisposed to rise. However, her indisposition was overcome, and in the course of twenty minutes or so she appeared arrayed in a frigid dignity and a loose wrapper. Rose, meanwhile, had taken off her curl papers, and Jaune regarded her tumbled hair with ecstasy.

The tribunal being assembled, the prisoner was placed at the bar and the trial began. It was an eminently irregular trial, looking at it from a legal point of view, for the verbal evidence all was hearsay. But it also was extra legal in that it was brief and decisive. Brown gave his testimony in the shape of a repetition of the story that Jaune had told him had been told by Mr. Badger Brush's groom ; and when this was concluded, Jaune produced the jacket, razors, shears, and shaving brush, and stated the circumstances under which they had been found. Then the prosecution rested.

Being questioned by the court—that is to say, by Madame Carthame—in his own defence, the Count replied gloomily that he hadn't any. "When I saw that horse fellow," he said, "I knew that I was likely to get into trouble, and that was the reason why I wanted to get rid of these things. And now the game is up. It is all true. I was a barber. I am not a count. My real name is Stumps."

Then it was that Madame Carthame, blissfully ignorant of the fact that she had neglected to remove her night-cap, stood up in her place, with her wrapper gathered about her in a statuesque fashion, and in a tragic tone uttered the single word:

"Sortez!"

And the Count went!

Out, out into the chill and gloom of night went the false Count, never to return; and with him went Madame Carthame's fond hope that her daughter would be a countess, which also was the last barrier in the way of Jaune d'Antimoine's love. Perceiving that the force of fate inexorably was pressing upon her, Madame Carthame—still in her night-cap—bestowed upon Rose and Jaune the maternal blessing in a manner that, even allowing for the night-cap, was both stately and severe.

As at Vandyke Brown's wedding Jaune d'Antimoine was radiantly magnificent in " The Marquis Suit," adding splendor to the ceremony and rendering himself most pleasing in the eyes of Rose Carthame; so, a month later, he was yet more radiant when he wore the famous suit again, in the church of Saint Vincent de Paul, and was himself married.

Conté Crayon brought Mr. Badger Brush down to the wedding, and the groom came too, and the tailor got wind of it and came without being asked—and had to be implored not to work it up into an advertisement, as he very much wanted to do. Mrs. Vandyke

Brown, just home from her wedding journey, was the first — after the kiss of Madame Carthame had been sternly bestowed—to kiss the bride ; and Mr. Badger Brush irreverently whispered to Conté Crayon that he wished, by gad ! he had her chance !

ORPIMENT & GAMBOGE.

THE firm was in leather, down in the Swamp, and Mr. Orpiment used to ride down-town every morning from his house in Bank Street, regular as the almanac, in a Bleecker Street car. His house was one of those eminently respectable, high-stooped dwellings, between Fourth Street and the old Greenwich Road—quite the court end of what used to be Greenwich village three score years or so ago, and about as pleasant an abiding-place as you will find to-day in all the city of New York. This house was unnecessarily large for Mr. Orpiment's family—for the whole of his family was himself; but as he seemed to be entirely satisfied with it, no one ventured to suggest to him that he had better move. Indeed, there were few people in the world who, knowing Mr. Orpiment, would have willingly ventured to suggest to him anything whatever, for he was not a person who took suggestions kindly. In point of fact, he usually took them with a snap.

When young Orpiment, in a suggestive sort of way, observed modestly from under his blonde mustache that his uncle would be doing a good thing if he would rescind the edict under which he, young Orpiment, was going through the form of learning the leather business, and would permit him to betake himself to the study of Art—when young Orpiment made this suggestion, I say, Mr. Orpiment fell into such a rage that his counting-house—large though it was and small though he was—would not hold him; in his wrath he strode out into his warehouse, among the kips and hides, and used language in their presence strong enough to tan them. The upshot of the matter was, that young Orpiment was given twenty-four hours in which to make up his mind whether he would stick to leather and his bread and butter, or be an infernal idiot (such was Mr. Orpiment's unparliamentary language) and starve among his paint-pots. And young Orpiment, his crisp blonde hair fairly bristling with determination, every muscle in his large, well-built body tense with energy, in something less than twenty-four seconds elected for starvation and the pots of paint.

But for all his high temper and defiant way of dealing with things, there was one thing that Mr. Orpiment could not deal with defiantly. One morning—only a few weeks after this battle royal of the paint-pots had been fought—to the astonishment of all the people in Bank Street, his front door did not open at precisely twenty-seven minutes after eight o'clock; and the conductor of the Bleecker Street car concluded that in some mysterious way he must have got ahead of his schedule, because at 8.30 Mr. Orpiment was not standing, like a block-signal, with his neatly-folded umbrella thrust out straight before him, at the Bank Street crossing; and Mr. Gamboge got into a nervous fluster, and said that he knew that something must be wrong, when the counting-house clock struck nine and Mr. Orpiment did not make his appearance, as was his invariable custom, between the sixth stroke and the seventh. And something *was* wrong: Mr. Orpiment was dead.

As all through his life Mr. Orpiment had been setting himself to go off, like an alarm clock, at definitely determined points in the future, so did he carry this habit into the testamentary disposition of his estate. His will, so to speak, was double-barrelled. The first barrel went off immediately upon his decease, and, as it were, set the alarm. After devising certain small legacies to a few friends and dependants, to be paid out of accruing income, and a round ten thousand dollars in Government bonds to the Protestant Home for Half-Orphans—an institution in which, for many years, Mr. Orpiment had taken the liveliest interest, probably because in his early life he had been a half-orphan himself, and knew how very disagreeable it was; after these rational and commendable bequests, the will took a new departure, and the rest of it was as eccentric and as arbitrary as ever Mr. Orpiment himself had been : and that is saying a good deal.

It declared that all the rest, residue, and remainder of Mr. Orpiment's estate, real and personal, whatsoever and wheresoever, was given, devised, and bequeathed unto his executors—Mr. Gamboge and Mr. Mangan Brown were the executors—in trust : to collect and receive the income thereof, and to pay thereout all necessary charges and expenses, and to invest the surplus income each year, and to add the same to the principal of Mr. Orpiment's estate, and thus to reinvest and accumulate for the period of five years after Mr. Orpiment's decease; and at the expiration of the said period, to hold the said principal, with its additions and accumulations, upon the further trusts set out in a codicil to this Mr. Orpiment's will, which codicil would be found in the top drawer of the small fire-proof safe in Mr. Orpiment's library; and (here was the queerest part of all) that until the expiration of the said five years this codicil was not to be opened under any circumstances whatsoever. The will further provided that until the five years should be ended Mr. Gamboge should carry on the business of the firm under the firm name; and, in an extremely peremptory clause, he was forbidden to give employment, in any shape or way, to young Orpiment. The leather business and the art business, the will stated dryly, were inharmonious; and inasmuch as young Orpiment had chosen the latter, the testator wished to leave him entirely free to carry it on undisturbed by the claims of the former upon his thought and time.

With this parting shot the will ended, as a sailor would say, short—without giving, save as such was to be found in the tidy legacy to the Protestant half-orphans, the least hint or suggestion as to what was to become of Mr. Orpiment's fortune at the end of the five years; without throwing the faintest ray of light upon the mystery that all this waiting and trust-creating involved. It was as queer a will as ever went to probate ; indeed, had there been anybody besides young Orpiment to contest it, the probabilities are that it would not have been admitted to probate at all. But young Orpiment was Mr. Orpiment's sole kinsman ; and, as matters stood just then, his pride was so thoroughly up that had he been called upon to choose between breaking the will and breaking his own neck, he would have chosen the latter alternative with all possible celerity.

And so, although he was dead and buried, Mr. Orpiment had arranged matters in such a fashion that for these five years at least it by no means could be said with any sort of truthfulness that he had perished from off the earth.

About this time there was not a happier family in all Greenwich, nor anywhere else, for that matter, than the Browns. Mr. Mangan Brown, in the large-hearted way that became his big body and big voice, and acting, of course, with the warm approval of Miss Caledonia, had urged Vandyke and Rose so heartily to bring the baby and come and live with them, that a refusal really was quite out of the question. So it came to pass that Mr. Mangan Brown, without the perceptible quiver of so much as an eyelash, signed a check big enough to pay for one of those delightful houses, with gardens in front of them, and broad verandas all the way up to their third stories, in West Eleventh Street— which also is a part of Greenwich village, as may be mentioned for the information of the mass of New Yorkers who know nothing of New York.

And in this pretty home, one bright May day, when the trees and gardens were glad in their fresh loveliness of delicious green, they all harmoniously took up their abode. Mr. Mangan Brown had the second-story front, and Miss Caledonia and Verona had the two second-story backs, and the third floor was given over to the baby and Vandyke and Rose. If anything could make brighter the bright spring-time, it was the sight of Rose and the baby on the veranda in the early morning sunlight—Rose, prettier than ever, laughing delightedly at the baby's earnest efforts to reach out over the row of flower-pots and clutch the swaying branches of the trees. Before going to his big studio on Fourteenth Street, to begin the work of the day, Van liked to smoke his after-break-fast pipe on the veranda and contemplate this pretty picture.

In the two years which had slipped away since his marriage a good deal more than he ever had dared even to hope for had come to pass. Thanks to his own pluck and hard work, which had won for him Uncle Man-gan's substantial backing, he now was as suc-cessful an artist as there was to be found in all New York. At times, in contemplation of his good fortune, he was rather more than half inclined to think that he must be some-body else ; an excess of mysticism that Rose resolutely refused to countenance—for in such a case to whom was she married? she pertinently asked. As for Mr. Mangan Brown, from being rather a grumpy sort of an old fellow, he had come to be positively beaming—a sort of overgrown fairy god-father, as it were, to the whole household. Not even the most remote allusion did he now make to the commercial rather than natural genesis of Miss Caledonia's back hair: and by this sign Miss Caledonia knew that he had experienced a change of heart. Moreover, he was instant in good works to each of the several members of the family; indeed, the extraordinary gifts which he constantly brought home to little Madder (named for his grandfather, of course) kept Rose constantly in a condition between laughter and tears.

"What can Madder possibly do with a grindstone, Uncle Mangan?"

"Possibly nothing at present, my dear. But I remember when I was a boy and lived in the country, I wanted a grindstone more than anything else in the world—especially after old Mitre Rabbit, the wheelwright, you know, said that I couldn't use his; and I am sure that Madder will be glad enough, when he is a little older, to have one of his own. It can go in the cellar until he wants it, and in the mean time it will be useful to sharpen the carving knife."

Rose shuddered as her imagination conjured up a ghastly picture of Madder more or less cut to pieces with the knives which the grindstone had made cruelly sharp; and she registered a mental vow that only over her dead body should her offspring ever come into possession of this shocking gift.

Now two of the most constant of the rather numerous visitors to this exceptionally happy household were young Orpiment and Mr. Gamboge. All the way along for the past twenty years or so, Mr. Gamboge had been in the habit of spending one or two evenings in each and every week in company with Mr. Mangan Brown—his friend and also his associate in trade. Mr. Gamboge and Mr. Mangan Brown had known each other ever since they were boys; and M. Brown & Co., and Orpiment & Gamboge owned in partnership a tannery in Lycoming County, Pennsylvania, and in various other directions the interests of the two firms were identical. Ostensibly, the visits of Mr. Gamboge were for the purpose of quietly and comfortably talking over the affairs of the tannery; but it was an open secret—in part revealed by the exceptionally careful brushing bestowed upon his fuzzy, close-cropped, grayish hair, by the exceeding smoothness of his smooth-shaven, fresh-colored face, by the admirable precision of the cut and fit of his neat black clothes—that their real object was Miss Caledonia. And there was a pleasant twinkle in his kindly gray eyes when they happened to meet—as they very often did—Miss Caledonia's kindly brown ones, that made this open secret more open still.

In point of fact, for nearly the full term of the twenty years during which Mr. Gamboge had been making his weekly visits, he had held toward Miss Caledonia the somewhat trying position of an earnest but undeclared lover. His earnestness could not for a moment be doubted; but although Miss Caledonia—in a strictly proper and maidenly manner, be it understood—had contrived that he should have at least one opportunity in each week during the past twenty years for making to her a formal tender of the heart that she well knew without such tender was hers, it was a melancholy fact that each of these ten hundred and forty opportunities successively had been wasted.

"Did he say anything to-night, Caledonia?"

"No, brother, not to-night. I think—I think that next week——"

"Um. Possibly. Good-night, Caledonia."

"Good-night, brother."

This conversation between Mr. Mangan Brown and Miss Caledonia had come to be stereotyped. Before Mr. Mangan experienced his change of heart this was the occasion that he usually took for referring to the commercial characteristics of her back hair in terms as pointed as they were unkind. And not seldom would he go even further, and advise that Miss Caledonia should investigate into the requirements precedent to admission into Saint Luke's Home for Aged Couples, on Hudson Street—assuring her that if ever she and Mr. Gamboge got so far along as to want a home for couples of any sort, this certainly would be the only home at all suited to their needs. Many and many a night, her night-cap being drawn well down over the thinly-thatched region that was covered luxuriantly by the hair of commerce by day, did Miss Caledonia fall asleep with tears in her gentle brown eyes and heaviness in her heart. But, being a round little woman of sanguine temperament, she managed on the whole to keep up her courage pretty well Each week, when Mr. Gamboge meaningly pressed her plump little hand as he bade her good-night, yet left still unsaid what he had come expressly to say, she believed that the next week would see his moral strength established firmly at last ; that then the words would be spoken which he so earnestly longed to utter, and which she so earnestly longed to hear. And so believing, Miss Caledonia lived on always in hope.

Now the trouble with Mr. Gamboge that made him keep silence in this provoking fashion was a constitutional indecision that he could in nowise overcome. Never did there live a man with less of positiveness in his nature than Mr. Gamboge had in his. This was the reason why he and Mr. Orpiment always had got along so well together. Mr. Orpiment, on the shortest notice, could be positive enough about anything for six ordinary people, and upon this superabundance of resolution Mr. Gamboge was accustomed to draw in order to make good his own lack. Indeed, he could not have adopted any other line of conduct without getting into difficulties, for Mr. Orpiment, as is the way with positive people the world over, could not tolerate even the most remote approach to positiveness on the part of anybody else. He might admit, perhaps, though certainly disdainfully, that in the abstract two or more opinions might be entertained upon a given subject; but the moment that the matter became concrete, his view narrowed into the unalterable conviction that there was just one single tenable opinion concerning it—and that was his. And, if peace was to be preserved, that opinion had to be adopted in a hurry. Mr. Gamboge, whose love of peace was so great that it was the only thing in the world that he would have fought for, always adopted his partner's opinions with a becoming alacrity. Nor did he, while Mr. Orpiment's convictions were in course of formation, venture to have any of his own. If appealed to under such conditions, his answer invariably was: "I am waiting to confer with Mr. Orpiment." And upon the rare occasions when, in some matter foreign to the affairs of the firm, he ventured so far as to express views distinctively his own, it had come to be his habit to preface his remarks with some such phrase as " Under these conditions, I think that Mr. Orpiment would say," or, " In a case of this sort, I think that Mr. Orpiment would do." The fact was observed, however, by people who knew both the members of the firm well, that what Mr. Gamboge thus said or did under the supposititious shelter of Mr. Orpiment's mantle, usually had a deal more of quiet good sense about it than probably would have been manifested had the matter really been settled by Mr. Orpiment himself.

For some time after that morning when Mr. Orpiment stayed at home and died in his bed instead of coming down-town in the Bleecker Street car, the habit of referring to his late partner's opinions increased upon Mr. Gamboge greatly. Not a hide, not even a kip, did he buy or sell without having something to say to the seller or buyer as to what Mr. Orpiment would have thought about the terms upon which the transaction was concluded. But again it was observed by certain long-headed leather-men down in the Swamp, that since the decease of the senior partner the firm of Orpiment & Gamboge was doing a much larger and also a much safer business than ever it had done while the very positive Mr. Orpiment was alive.

However, the habit of a life-time cannot be given over in a day. It is true that Mr. Gamboge, now that Mr. Orpiment was buried and done for, was beginning gradually to have a few opinions and a trifling amount of positiveness of his own; but as yet it was all too soon to expect him to possess, still less to act upon, a positive opinion touching this momentous matter of his own heart and Miss Caledonia's hand.

As to the other visitor at the Brown's, young Orpiment, matters were entirely different. With an energetic promptness that was strictly in keeping with the traditions of his family, he had declared his love for Verona under the most unfavorable circumstances and in the most unmistakable terms. With a disregard of prudence and reason that was positively heroic, he had made this avowal on the very day that his uncle had bidden him begone to his paint-pots and starve. Whether he thought that love, being had in sufficient quantities, would make starvation impossible, or that if he must starve it would be pleasanter to do it in loving company, I am not prepared to say; but it is a fact that in less than three hours after he had, as he put it, disinherited his uncle, he had asked Verona Brown to marry him—and Verona Brown, collapsing from the pinnacle of dignity upon which usually she was exalted, suffered her beautiful dark hair to be shockingly tumbled upon young Orpiment's shoulder, and, with infinite tenderness and infinite love in her sweet, low voice, told him very frankly that she would!

There was a suggestion, at least, of poetic justice in this reckless entanglement of Verona's affections by young Orpiment; for it was Vandyke Brown who had been very largely the cause of the entanglement of young Orpiment's affections by the goddess

Art, to the utter ruin of his exceptionally brilliant prospects in the leather business. Young Orpiment had artistic talent, possibly artistic genius, and Brown had the wit to perceive it. Without thinking of the harm that he might be doing, he urged young Orpiment to abandon the leather that he hated and to give himself to the art that he loved; and it was not until his advice was taken, and he was called upon to behold the pretty kettle of fish that had come of it, that he perceived what a serious responsibility the giving of advice involves. With his own dreary experience still fresh in mind, he realized far more clearly than young Orpiment did, or could, how nearly hopeless is the struggle for artistic success when the artist has to earn his daily bread as he goes along. But he kept these cheerful reflections to himself—that is to say, to himself and Rose. They were quite agreed that young Orpiment and Verona had a sufficiency of troubles in hand without being called upon to take any upon interest.

To be sure, there was a ray of hope for a moment when Mr. Orpiment died, for young Orpiment was his legal and only heir. But this hope was promptly extinguished, or pretty nearly so, by Mr. Orpiment's extraordinary double-barrelled will—with that ominous legacy in the first barrel to the Protestant half-orphans.

"It will be just like the old wretch to have left those miserable half-orphans every cent of his money, Van," said Rose with energetic determination. "And a nice thing that will be, to be sure ; turning all their heads by making so many millionaires of them ! "

"The 'ome 'alf-orphan," observed Jaune d'Antimoine, who happened to be present when Rose thus freed her mind. "Ah, 'e is the estabelisment most curious in Tens Street. I 'ave much vondered at 'im. Tell me, my Van, what is this 'ome 'alf-orphan ? "

"It's a place where they take care of children born with only one leg and one arm. Of course, children like that have to be taken care of by somebody. It's a capital charity. We'll go down there some day and see 'em. They're a jolly queer lot; all go about hopping, you know."

"Nonsense, Van. Don't believe him, M. d'Antimoine. They are called half-orphans because they have only one father or one mother. I'm a half-orphan myself."

"Eh? But, truly, Madame Brown, it is not most common for the child to 'ave more than one father or one mother—not, that is, is it thought well that 'e should 'ave more. Ah, pardon! I forget that Madame says that she is 'erself 'alf-orphan. No doubt to be so is most well in this country. In America is not as in France."

M. d'Antimoine no more comprehended why Brown went off into such fits of laughter, nor why Rose blushed a little and laughed too, than he did the laborious explanation of the constituent elements of a half-orphan that Brown, under the circumstances, felt called upon to make to him.

But whether Mr. Orpiment's money was

9

or was not destined for the use of this excellent charity, there was no ground for hoping that any part of it was destined for his nephew; the spiteful clause in the will forbidding Mr. Gamboge to give employment to young Orpiment cut hope in this direction short off. Obviously, this clause was put in to serve as a check upon any indiscretion that Mr. Gamboge might be led into by what Mr. Orpiment always had styled his absurdly soft heart; and it was a patent declaration of a tolerably positive sort that young Orpiment was disinherited. His sole fortune, under these circumstances, was a little property that had come down to him from his father, and that yielded him the magnificent income of four hundred and seventy-one dollars a year. However, this was enough to keep a roof over his head, and to feed him and to give him at very long intervals something in the way of new clothes. Mr. Gamboge, by artfully representing the solitariness of his own home, did his best to make young Orpiment come and share it with him ; but his uncommonly tall stories about his melancholy loneliness — stories, let us hope, which were promptly blotted out in the celestial account against him by the friendly tears of the recording angel—did not deceive his auditor. Gratefully, but decidedly, the tender thus made of exceedingly comfortable free quarters was declined. But the invitations to dinner that Mr. Gamboge and the Browns showered upon him could not be refused—at least not without giving pain ; and so, while his raiment was anything but purple and fine linen, young Orpiment at least fared sumptuously pretty nearly every day. And he was cheered and comforted, as only the love of a good woman can cheer and comfort a man, by the love of Verona Brown.

Verona certainly manifested a most conspicuous lack of worldly wisdom in thus lavishing her affections upon a man whose fortunes were so near to being desperate. But then—excepting in the case of Mr. Mangan—worldly wisdom was not a prominent characteristic of the Brown family ; and even Mr. Mangan had less of it now than he had before he experienced his change of heart.   Only a couple of years earlier in his life, acting in the capacity of Verona's guardian, he would have shown young Orpiment to the door with amazing promptitude and energy, had he ventured to present himself, under such circumstances as at present existed, in the guise of Verona's suitor. And, in truth, he had no great liking for what was going on now; but now, at least, he took a larger, a more liberal view of life than had been his habit in the past—for the lesson that he had learned from his relations with Van had made him more tolerant. Therefore it was that, instead of heaping maledictions upon young Orpiment's head, he ordered a landscape from him.   In due time this order was filled, and the picture was sent home.   There was ever so much of it, and its light and shade were ever so queer, and there was something dreadfully wrong in its perspective ; but, for all its eccentricities, there were in it hints of genuine good quality. It was a harrowing thing of look at, of course ; but its badness was the badness of a crudity in which there was hope.

So they had young Orpiment to dinner, and after dinner the picture was hung solemnly over the mantel-piece in the front parlor. This was an honorable position for it to occupy, and it was a position that possessed certain practical advantages ; for when the gas was lighted, unless you climbed over one of the diagonally placed sofas and got quite into one of the corners of the room, the picture had such a glitter upon it that it simply was invisible. Old Madder, who also was dining with them that night, began to comment upon this fact—and only made matters worse by asking Rose, in an aggrieved tone, what he was saying that he shouldn't say to make her pinch him so.

Of course this was not a genuine sale, looking at the matter from an artist's standpoint ; and certain other sales—to Mr. Gamboge and to some of the friends of these two purchasers—were not genuine either; but they served their well-meant purpose of keeping the fire going under the pot that young Orpiment so gallantly was striving to make boil.

Old Madder, by the way, much enjoyed dining with the young people, and they and Mr. Mangan and Miss Caledonia made him very welcome. At these dinners he conducted himself upon the lines of a serious dignity, and seriously talked art to Mr. Mangan, whose knowledge of art was limited to a commercial appreciation of the value of gilt decorations on red leather boot-tops designed for the Western trade; or, when he happened to be in a cantankerous mood, made vicious thrusts at Van and the young geniuses generally, under the guise of lamentations over the degeneracy of modern painters. His own work, of course, continued to be as exasperating as ever. He nearly drove Van wild by insisting upon painting a portrait of little Madder, that was hung on the line at the Academy, and that was described in the catalogue as "Grandfather's Darling." From the degenerate modern painters with whom he associated, Van did not hear the last of that horrible caricature of his first-born for years. Among the League men the picture was styled " The Slaughter of the Innocent "—which naturally enough led somebody to speak of the artist as Herod, and so won for old Madder the nickname of Herod Madder that he bore, without knowing it, to the end of his days. After this bitter experience, when old Madder wanted to paint Rose and the new baby, little Caledonia (to all intents and purposes his " Soldier's Widow and Orphaned Child " over again), and call it " The Young Mother's First Love," Brown put his foot down firmly and said that it should not be done. And not until several months had passed—in the course of which old Madder gradually had convinced himself that Brown was jealous of his superior work, and that, under these circumstances, he could afford to be magnanimous — did old Madder and Brown get along well together again.

By the time that this second baby was born, Brown had conquered so firm a standing-place, and was so crowded with work that his acceptance of an order had come to be considered something of a favor. Young Orpiment, being present one day when an order actually was rejected, and knowing that Brown had fought and won just such a battle as he was fighting, felt himself stirred with hope.

And, in truth, as the season of his apprenticeship wore away, there came to be a good deal for young Orpiment to feel hopeful about. Working steadily and earnestly, the weeks and the months slipped by until he found behind him, since the day when he forswore Leather as a master and took for his mistress Art, three whole years; and three years of honest hard work, if a man has got anything in him to begin with, is bound to tell. His little pictures — after those first orders he had the sense not to paint big ones—had a fair sale now on their merits. They did not sell for much, it is true, and they still were a long way off from being really good work; but at least the good quality that was in them no longer was obscured by bad perspective and by doubtful light and shade. They had a clear, fresh tone, moreover, that was distinctively their own. Being sent to the exhibitions, they no longer were rejected; and some of the more recent ones had taken a most encouraging step downward from the sky toward the line. The newspapers began to mention his work respectfully, and *The Skeptic,* with an amiable exercise of its powers of prophecy based upon its faculty for recognizing genius in embryo, even went so far as to say that in him another landscape painter had been born.

All this was tremendously encouraging, of course, and young Orpiment was heartened and comforted by it greatly; but even with such good fortune attending him, he could not but find weariness in his long time of waiting for an income from his work that would enable him to make Verona his wife. Both Mr. Mangan Brown and Mr. Gamboge had offered repeatedly to discount for him the future that now pretty certainly was his; but this good offer, with Verona's entire approval, he decidedly refused. If Verona would wait for him while he worked, he said —and the light of a strong resolution shone in his blue eyes—he would work on until his success was won. And Verona, with the gentle dignity that was natural to her, drew up her tall, graceful figure to its full height, and answered simply that she would wait— would wait, she said, and without the least intention of irony, for forty years.

For these expectant lovers, the example set them by Miss Caledonia and Mr. Gamboge was most encouraging. What was their three years of probation in comparison with the three-and-twenty years of probation that their elders had endured? And the encouragement thus given was all the greater because, as time went on, the matrimonial prospects of Mr. Gamboge and Miss Caledonia apparently stood still. In the past three years Miss Caledonia had contrived near eight-score fresh opportunities for the long-delayed proposal ; and on each of these several occasions Mr. Gamboge had hesitated until his opportunity was lost. On the whole, however, Miss Caledonia's sanguine nature found cause for encouragement in the perceptible change that had come over Mr. Gamboge as these three years sped by. No less than twice, to her certain knowledge, had he expressed positively a positive opinion of his own. On a memorable Saturday he had said, in a firm voice, before the whole family assembled at the dinner-table, that rare roast beef was much improved by horse-radish. On a memorable Thursday evening he had said, addressing Mr. Mangan Brown, and in a tone of bold effrontery that thrilled her soul with joy, that " this idiotic tinkering at the tariff on foreign leather was simply unpardonable." On neither of these occasions did Mr. Gamboge refer even remotely to Mr. Orpiment : not a word about Mr. Orpiment's preferences in the matter of applying horse-radish to roast beef; not a word about Mr. Orpiment's opinions in regard to the customs duties on foreign hides. Here was living proof that Mr. Gamboge was getting to have a will of his own; and here, consequently, was substantial ground upon which Miss Caledonia could found her conviction that a happy ending to her long courting was near at hand.

Nor was this all. To the best of Miss Caledonia's belief, Mr. Gamboge actually once had got so far as to make a real start toward speaking the momentous words which would resolve into a glad certainty their three-and-twenty years of doubt. It was upon a pleasant Sunday afternoon in the late spring-time that Mr. Gamboge got started— in the mellow weather when the buds of May were bursting into the blossoms of June, and all nature was glad with the bright promise of the coming summer's generous life. They two were seated alone upon the veranda, screened from the too-curious gaze of passers-by by festoons of the climbing plants which had shot up blithely since the warm days began ; and Mr. Gamboge, in a state of post-prandial contentment, was smoking an especially satisfactory cigar. After the fashion of a dove-like serpent, Miss Caledonia by degrees had shifted the ground of their talk until it had come to be of the dreary life that Mr. Gamboge was leading in his great house wherein he dwelt alone. There was a tender solicitude in Miss Caledonia's tone that sunk deep into the heart of Mr. Gamboge and wrought great havoc there. Her low, gentle voice sounded sweetly in his ears ; her suggestions for his comfort were practical without being revolutionary ; he felt—but more keenly than ever before in all the twenty-three years—that in Miss Caledonia he would find a helpmate indeed. His excellent dinner—prepared, as he well knew, under Miss Caledonia's supervision—his excellent cigar, the soft spring weather, Miss Caledonia's pleasingly plump person and sympathetic words: all these agreeable forces, acting upon his newly acquired disposition to have a will of his own and to use it, conspired to make him utter the decisive words. A nervous thrill went over him, and he straightened himself in his chair. Miss Caledonia saw what was coming, and was struck with awe. She ceased speaking; her hands fluttered with her handkerchief; there was a trembling of her lips.

"In regard to our personal relations, Miss Caledonia, I am sure that Mr. Orpiment would have said—that is, I know that under these conditions Mr. Orpiment would have done—in fact, I am confident that Mr. Orpiment would have approved——"

"Oh, confound old Orpiment," said that wretched Vandyke Brown, stepping out upon the veranda through the open window in time to hear this last mention of Mr. Orpiment's name. "Of course you know, Mr. Gamboge," he went on, "I don't want to hurt your feelings, or anything"—for he saw that Mr. Gamboge was very much upset—

" But when I think what a lot of good that old screw might have done by leaving his money to his nephew, and so giving him a fair start in the world, I really can't help hating the very sound of his name.

" Aunt Caledonia, Rose wants to know if you can tell what on earth has gone with Madder's light cloak. You had him out yesterday, you know, and Rose can't find it anywhere."

" You will find it where it belongs," answered Miss Caledonia frigidly, " on the third shelf of the closet in the back room."

And so good fortune had come sailing down over the sea of hope to Miss Caledonia —even had stopped to signal her—and then had sailed away ! After that rude interruption the perturbed spirit of Mr. Gamboge— although Miss Caledonia did her best to bring it—could not be brought back to the tender mood that so fairly had promised a fair solution of the long-vexed problem of their lives. Still, having come thus close to happiness, Miss Caledonia felt more than ever certain that happiness yet would be hers.

So the months went rolling on and on, and the time drew near when Mr. Orpiment's five years' lease upon posterity would end. Under the judicious management of Mr. Gamboge, his late partner's estate had increased prodigiously, and the prospects of the Protestant half-orphans were amazingly fine.

"I don't doubt that the miserable little creatures will get fifty thousand dollars apiece—and I hope that it will choke them ! " said Rose in a fine burst of indignation and in a fine mixture of metaphors. Nothing that Van could say could convince Rose that Mr. Orpiment's property would not be divided up among the individual half-orphans in the asylum at the time when the bequest became operative.

As to young Orpiment, he really did not care very much now whether the half-orphans got his uncle's money or not. He was fairly on his legs by this time, with a steady income of two thousand dollars or so a year, and he and Verona were to be married very soon. Of course, they would have to live in a very quiet way, and some of the things which they most wanted to do—the trip to the glorious mountain region of Northern New Mexico, for instance—would have to wait awhile. But the great point was that at last he was earning enough by his own work to permit him, without utterly defying Mr. Mangan Brown and worldly wisdom, to make Verona his wife.

For young Orpiment had fought bravely and had won gallantly his battle for the standard of Art. And wasn't Verona proud of him, though! For Verona knew that his fight for success as an artist was only the visible form of his fight for success as a lover; and all the wealth of her strong love, all her honoring esteem, went out to this her hero, who, for her love's sake, had conquered the world!

With the solemnity befitting so decisive

an occasion, Mr. Gamboge wrote a formal
invitation to young Orpiment to be present,
on the fifth anniversary of the day after the
day of Mr. Orpiment's death, at the going
off of the second barrel of Mr. Orpiment's
will.   But, in order to mitigate the formality
a little, and to make somewhat less solemn
the solemnity, Mr. Gamboge himself handed
the written invitation to young Orpiment,
and added to it a verbal invitation to come
and dine with him as a preliminary to the
reading.   Under the circumstances, the fact
was obvious that Verona had a constructive
right to be present when the will was read;
and as Verona could not with propriety be
present alone, the necessity presented itself
of asking Miss Caledonia to come with her.
Naturally, this suggested the advisability of
asking Mr. Mangan Brown too.   And having got this far, Mr. Gamboge concluded
that he might just as well go a little farther
and ask Van and Rose and old Madder; and
so he did.

It was only a lucky accident, however,

that saved the party from being entirely broken up by a rash act of little Caledonia's. Van wanted Rose's hands for something that he was painting, and she had gone up to the studio the day before the will dinner-party —as she styled the feast that Mr. Gamboge was to give—taking the baby along with her. There was not much of this baby, and she was not quite two years old, but she had a faculty for getting into pickles far beyond her size and years. However, there did not seem to be much chance for her to get into trouble on the studio floor.

The fact must be confessed that, although they had been married for five years, Rose and Van had a shocking habit of philandering ; and so it fell out, when he had put in her hands to his satisfaction, that he had laid down his palette and brushes on the foot of his easel, and somehow they had drifted into the big chair, and had got to talking about that autumn morning when " Lydia Darragh " perished, and the great happiness of their lives began.

" It was dreadful, Van, the way that I told you, right out before all those men, that I loved you !   I never can think of it without blushing." (Rose was blushing most charmingly, and that was a fact.)   " But I really never thought of them at all, and that's the solemn truth.   All that I thought of was your ruined work, and of what you were working for—it was me that you were working for, you know, and I knew all about it ! —and of trying to comfort you.   *Did* it comfort you, dear ?   Are you *sure*, Van, that you are glad that you married me ?   Have I *really* made you happy?   You are so good to me ——

" Caledonia ! *Caledonia !* STOP ! Merciful heaven, Van, she's got your palette and is eating the paints ! Our child is poisoned ! She will die !" And Rose shot up, much as she would have done had Van been a catapult and suddenly gone off, and caught the chromnivorous infant in her arms.

Van was pretty badly scared too, but he had his wits about him, and looked at the palette before giving his assent to Rose's alarmed proposition that death by poison must be the inevitable result of Caledonia's unnatural repast.

"Steady, Rose. I guess it's all right. She's begun at the black end of the palette, luckily, and she's eaten only as far as asphaltum. No doubt she'll have a lively time in her little inside, but she hasn't had a scrap of the light colors, and there's nothing in the dark ones to damage her much. But we'd better rush her off to the doctor, all the same."

And Van was right. Caledonia did not perish, but she had a tremendously large stomach-ache for so small a stomach, and she kept her bed for the remainder of the day. Mr. Mangan Brown, in a well-meant endeavor to mitigate the severity of her sufferings, the very next morning bought her a concertina, and a pair of skates, and a richly illustrated octavo Life of Washington. That these appropriate gifts inured to her betterment is problematical, but she certainly was so completely recovered by the ensuing evening that her illness was no barrier to the success of the will dinner-party given by Mr. Gamboge.

The dinner in every way was admirable —although Miss Caledonia secretly noticed certain shortcomings in the service, which she promptly resolved should be corrected when she was called upon to take command. But for all the excellence of the dinner, the assembled company was disposed to slight it—to hurry through with it in order to get at the reading of the will. Even the fact that young Orpiment on that very day had sold his big picture, " Spring on the Hudson Highlands," for $450—the highest price that anything of his so far had brought— scarcely made a ripple upon the strong stream of curiosity that was sweeping forward toward the moment when positive knowledge would determine what part the Protestant half-orphans were to play in the final disposition of Mr. Orpiment's estate.

" If it wasn't for Verona, he might pick

out the nicest looking of the girl half-orphans for a wife, and get part of it back that way," said Rose under her breath to Van, as they passed from the dining-room to the library, where Mr. Gamboge was to read the will. "But as things are, though," she added with a touch of melancholy in her tone, "that is quite out of the question."

"What would be even better," Van answered seriously, "would be for him to drop Verona, turn Mormon, and marry 'em all. Then he'd bag half of it, anyway."

"Of course you all know," said Mr. Gamboge in a slightly oratorical tone, holding the sealed will in his hand, "that I have no knowledge whatever of the contents of this document. Should its contents be what I fear they are, you all know that I shall feel, as you all will feel, that a great injustice has been done to our young and gifted friend; to our friend, who by his noble force of character, not less than by his great genius—"

"Don't," said young Orpiment, appealingly.

"Well, I won't," said Mr. Gamboge, dropping suddenly from his oratorical heights. "But I will say this : if the estate don't come to you, my dear boy, I shall think less of Mr. Orpiment's judgment then I ever did— and I never did think much of it, anyway."

At these spirited words Miss Caledonia's heart gave a bound—for she perceived that now, beyond a doubt or a peradventure, Mr. Gamboge had come into the kingdom of his personal independence at last : and she was his waiting queen! As for Mr. Mangan Brown, his lower jaw dropped as though the muscles had parted ; and Van gave utterance to a prolonged whistle that Rose had the presence of mind to conceal by coughing violently.

Oblivious to the sensation caused by his revolutionary declaration, Mr. Gamboge adjusted his spectacles, broke the three black seals, and began the reading of the will. It set out with the affirmation that Mr. Orpiment feared God and was in his right mind —statements which caused Miss Caledonia to purse her lips together doubtingly—and went on with a list of the testator's possessions : the house in which he had lived, and some other houses ; his share in the tannery in Lycoming County, Pennsylvania ; some warehouses down-town ; some building lots on Seventy-ninth Street ; various stocks and bonds ; and his interest in the leather business carried on by the firm of Orpiment & Gamboge.

" I wonder how the half-orphans will settle about the houses and building lots ? " Rose whispered inquiringly as Mr. Gamboge paused at the end of the list.

" Draw lots for 'em, probably," Van whispered in reply.

Mr. Gamboge read on : " Whereas, by my will to which this codicil is supplement, I gave all my residuary estate to my executors upon certain trusts, now I appoint the further trusts referred to in said will as contained in this codicil."

At last Mr. Orpiment's intentions were to be made plain. Everybody bent forward, listening eagerly, and Mr. Gamboge could not keep his voice from trembling : " At the end of the said period of five years from the time of my decease I direct my executors to assign, convey, and pay over the whole of my residuary estate with its increase and accumulations to the person who, when the same is payable, shall act as treasurer to the Society for the Relief of Half-Orphan and Destitute Children in the City of New York, to be applied to the charitable uses and purposes of said society under its direction." Mr. Gamboge gave an audible groan, laid the will down on his knee, took off his spectacles, which suddenly had grown misty, and with his silk handkerchief wiped them dry.

" The unfeeling, unnatural, heartless old wretch ! " cried Rose.

" Never mind, dear ; you have conquered fortune for yourself, and I love you a thousand times more for it," said Verona in a low voice, as she took young Orpiment's hand in both of hers.

"It is shameful!" said Miss Caledonia.

"It is just what I expected," said Mr. Mangan Brown; "but I'm uncommonly sorry for you, all the same, Orpiment."

"It's all my fault, for leading you off into painting; I hope devoutly that you may live long enough to forgive me, old fellow," said Van, ruefully.

"Nonsense, Van. You've been the making of me, and I never can be sufficiently thankful to you," young Orpiment answered in a cheery tone that had a thoroughly genuine ring to it.

"Art alone is worth living for, Mr. Orpiment," said old Madder. "Because you have escaped the thralldom of riches, I congratulate you with all my heart!"

"There's another page of the thing," said Mr. Gamboge dismally, and making as he spoke a suspicious dab at his eyes with his big handkerchief. "We may as well get done with it," and he turned the page and read on:

"*Provided*, that at the end of said period

of five years from the time of my decease my nephew shall not have proved, by earning from the sale of his pictures an income of not less than $2,000 yearly; that in abandoning the leather business and in adopting the business of picture-painting, he was right in the choice of his vocation and I was wrong. Should this very improbable contingency arise, then at the time aforesaid I direct my executors to assign, convey, and pay over to him, my said nephew, the whole of my residuary estate with its increase and accumulations, to him, his heirs, executors, administrators, and assigns forever."

" God bless you, my dear boy!" fairly shouted Mr. Gamboge, dashing down the will and his spectacles and his handkerchief upon the floor, and rushing over to young Orpiment and hugging him. " God bless you, my dear boy, the estate really is yours after all!"

And everybody—everybody, that is, but Verona and old Madder—in the delight and excitement of the moment, followed Mr.

Gamboge's exhilarating example. Even the staid Mr. Mangan Brown, even the decorous Miss Caledonia, hugged young Orpiment as hard as ever they knew how. Verona just sat still and looked at him, and through the tears in her lovely brown eyes there shone the light of a great joy and the tenderness of a greater love. The thought that she also was a gainer by this revolution in young Orpiment's fortunes never once crossed her mind; all that she thought of was that his life of toil and struggle now was at an end; that for her hard-working hero the chance to do good work restfully had come at last.

(It was not until an hour or so later, when they were walking home together, that another phase of the matter presented itself to Rose—she was a great hand for seeing things in original lights. "Do you know, Van," she said in a very melancholy voice, "I can't help feeling dreadfully sorry for those poor little Protestant half-orphans? To think of their coming so near to being heirs and heiresses, and then not getting a single bit of their fortunes after all !")

Old Madder, waiting until the storm had subsided a little, and standing, as it were, afar off, did what he could to throw a wet blanket over the general joy by saying mournfully :

"I hope that this is for the best, Mr. Orpiment; but I fear that it is for the worst. Art is a jealous mistress, and Wealth is her sworn foe. You have my sincere pity, sir ; for I sincerely believe that you are a ruined man !"

However, old Madder's wet blanket was not a success, for his genial gloom no more could stay the eruption of happiness that had begun than a real wet blanket could stay an eruption of Vesuvius. Indeed, nobody paid the least attention to what he was saying, for just as he began his cheerful remarks Mr. Gamboge, looking rather nervous, but also looking very much resolved, rose to his feet with the air of a man who is about to make a speech. Somehow there was that in his manner that made all the blood in Miss Caledonia's body rush tumultuously to her heart. Her prophetic soul told her that it was coming now in very truth!

"My dear Brown," said Mr. Gamboge, addressing Mr. Mangan, "there is a matter very near to my heart, concerning which I long have desired to speak with you. Possibly you may have noticed that my attentions to your sister, Miss Caledonia, for some time past have been rather marked?"

"I have observed the phenomenon to which you refer," answered Mr. Mangan, for Mr. Gamboge had spoken interrogatively, and had paused for a reply—"I have observed the phenomenon to which you refer, my dear Gamboge, pretty constantly for the past twenty-five years."

"Precisely," said Mr. Gamboge, in a tone indicating that he felt encouraged. "You are right, my dear Brown, as you always are. My reckoning of the number of years during which my attentions to Miss Caledonia have been, as I say, rather marked corresponds with yours exactly. And it seems to me, my dear Brown, that this period has been of a sufficient extent to enable us—that is, to enable Miss Caledonia and me—to acquire such ample knowledge of each other's tastes, habits, and moral characteristics as will justify us in deciding now whether or not we prudently may advance to a yet closer relationship."

" Looking at the matter dispassionately, my dear Gamboge, I should say that it had."

" My own sentiments, my dear Brown, I may say, are, and for some years past have been, unalterably established. I revere your sister, Miss Caledonia, as the best and wisest of women. Under the existing circumstances, Mrs. Brown and Miss Verona will pardon, I am sure, this expression of what, under any other circumstances, might be considered, if not a too exalted, at least a too exclusive, estimate of her virtues."

" Certainly," said Rose.

" Of course," said Verona.

" Entertaining these unalterable sentiments, therefore, my dear Brown, the strongest, the holiest wish of my life is to make her my wife. To you, as her natural protector, to her, as the arbiter of her own destiny, I now appeal — on this auspicious occasion when my young friend Orpiment wears proudly in our presence his tripartite crown of riches, genius, and requited love. My dear Brown, may I have her? Miss Caledonia, will you be mine?"

" May he have you, Caledonia?"

" Oh, brother! how can you ask? It—it shall—be just as you say."

"Then I say, and I say it heartily, my dear Gamboge, take her—and God bless you both!" and Mr. Mangan Brown led the blushing Miss Caledonia to Mr. Gamboge and placed her hand in his.

11

And so, young Orpiment having come into his fortune, and Mr. Gamboge having come into his kingdom, Mr. Orpiment's lease upon posterity was cancelled, and he really was dead at last.

ROBERSON'S MEDIUM.

IT was Rowney Mauve who described Roberson as being like one of his own still-lifes : a lot of queer stuff badly composed and out of drawing, and with his perspective all wrong. And I regret to add that it was Miss Carmine, when she heard this description, and recognized its accuracy, who giggled. To say that Violet Carmine was a pickle, is presenting a statement of the case that is well within bounds.

The arrival of this somewhat erratic young person in New York was unexpected, and had a rather dramatic touch about it. On a warm evening in September, while yet the dying splendor of sunset hung redly over the Jersey Highlands, Mr. Mangan Brown was sitting in a wicker-chair on the veranda of his own exceedingly comfort-

able home in West Eleventh Street. He
was in the perfectly placid frame of mind
that is the right of a man who has dined
well, and who is smoking a good cigar.   In
another wicker-chair, similarly placid, similarly smoking a good cigar, sat Vandyke
Brown.   And between the two sat Rose:
whose nature was so sweet at all times, that
even after-dinner cigars (supposing that she
had been inclined to smoke them, and she
was not) could not have made it one particle
sweeter.   These three people were very
fond of each other: and they were talking
away pleasantly about nothing in particular,
and were gently light-hearted, and were
having a deal of enjoyment in a quiet way,
as they sat there, beneath their own vine
and ailanthus tree, in the light of the mellow after-glow left when the sun went down.
Their perfect peacefulness can be likened
only to that of a tropical calm : and, therefore, the unities of the situation were preserved, though its placidity was shattered,
when the calm was broken by what with a

tolerable degree of accuracy may be described as a tropical storm.

Out of a coupé, that stopped with a
flourish in front of Mr. Mangan Brown's
gate, descended a tall young woman, with
a good deal of color in her cheeks and a
good deal of black hair and a pair of exceptionally bright black eyes. She carried
a cage, in which was a large white cockatoo,
in one hand, and with the other she opened
the gate in a decisive sort of way, as though
she had a right to open it ; and in a positive,
proprietary fashion she traversed the walk
of flags to the veranda steps. Mr. Mangan
Brown arose from his wicker-chair—somewhat reluctantly, for he was very comfortable—and advanced to meet her.

"You must be my cousin Mangan. I
am very glad to see you, cousin Mangan.
Won't you take the parrot, please?" and
the young person held out the cage in her
left hand, and also extended her right hand
with the obvious purpose of having it
shaken.

Mr. Mangan Brown did his best to discharge simultaneously the two duties thus demanded of him, but as this involved crossing his hands in an awkward sort of way, the result was not altogether graceful. " My name *is* Mangan Brown," he said diplomatically.

" Of course it is," answered the young woman with a smile that showed what a charming mouth and what prodigiously fine teeth she had. " And my name is Violet Carmine. Don't you think Violet rather a pretty name, cousin Mangan ? My mamma gave it to me out of a novel. And don't you think that I speak very good English ? I haven't a strawberry mark on my left arm, nor anything like that, you know, to prove it, but I am your cousin, your second cousin once removed, just as much as though I had strawberry marks all over me. Don't look at me in that doubtful sort of way, cousin Mangan, it makes me feel quite uncomfortable. I'm sure if I am willing to believe in you, you might be willing to believe in me. But here's papa's letter ; just read it, and then you'll believe in me, I'm sure."

Mr. Mangan Brown, who was rather dazed by this assault, took the letter and began to read it.

"You're cousins, too, I suppose," said Miss Carmine, turning to Van and Rose. "Long cousin, won't you please go out to the carriage and pay the man and bring in my things?" As to you, you dear, little, blue-eyed cousin, I think that you are simply delightful, and I know that I shall love you with all my heart, and I must kiss you right away." And this Miss Carmine did with a fervor that was quite in keeping with the energy of her manner and words.

"I am very glad to see you, my dear," said Mr. Mangan Brown, who had finished the letter. "This is my nephew, Vandyke Brown, and this is his wife, my niece Rose, and I am sure that we all will do our best to make you comfortable while you stay with us. If—if I was not quite so cordial as I might have been just now, you must understand that your sudden arrival rather took me by surprise, you know. Rose, take your cousin Violet up to Caledonia's room, and make her comfortable. Van will carry up her bag."

" And, Rose dear," said Miss Carmine, precisely imitating Mr. Mangan's tone and manner, " take your cousin Violet to where she will get something to eat, please. I assure you that she is almost starving." In her own proper voice she continued : " You sweet, little, blue-eyed thing, it was worth while coming all the way from Mexico just to have a sight of you. You are a lucky fellow, Van. I don't believe you half deserve her. Tell the truth now, do you ? But, of course, he'll say yes, Rose, so we need not wait for his answer. Take me along, dear, and let me wash myself and get some food. You really have no idea how hungry I am." And Miss Carmine, with her arm around Rose's waist, vanished through the open door.

" Cool sort of hand, this cousin of ours," said Van to Mr. Mangan, when the bag and the parrot had been carried up-stairs and Van had come down again to the veranda. "And who is she, anyway? She really is our cousin, I suppose."

"Yes," said Mr. Mangan, in a tone that did its best to be cheerful, "there is no doubt about the relationship; though it certainly is rather a distant one. Her great-grandfather Carmine married my grandfather's, Bone Brown's, sister. Carmine had a cochineal plantation in San Domingo, and he was killed in the time of the insurrection. In fact, his slaves burnt him. His son got away and went over to Mexico, and the family has been there ever since. The present Carmine, Violet's father, has a big *hacienda* somewhere or another. We have a consignment of hides from him every year, and that's pretty much all that I know about him; except that in one of his letters he once said that he had married an American, and was bringing up his daughters—I don't think he has any sons—on the American plan; teaching them to be self-confident, and that sort of thing. And," continued Mr. Mangan reflectively, "if this young person is a fair specimen of the family, I should say that his educational methods had been, ah, quite a remarkable success."

"Yes," answered Van, dryly, "I think they have. But to what fortunate circumstance do we owe the pleasure of her descent upon our inoffensive household?"

"Don't be inhospitable, Van. I'm sure she's a nice girl, though she certainly is a little—a little odd, perhaps. Why, her father writes that he has sent her up to see something of American life under my care— he seems to take it for granted that I am married and have a lot of daughters—and when her visit is ended (he suggests that she shall stay with us for a year, or for six months at the least), he wants me to come down to his place with all my family and stay a year or so with him. It's Mexican, I suppose, visiting in this fashion. I always have understood that they did not make much account of time down there."

"But how on earth did she get here? Surely she did not come up alone?"

"Really, Van," said Violet, stepping out upon the veranda briskly, just in time to hear these questions. "Really, Van, you don't look stupid, but I think you must be. I came, sir, in a delightful Pullman car, and the Señor and Señora Moreno—I wonder if they can be distant relations of yours, cousin Mangan? It's the same name, you know—and all the thirteen, no, the fourteen, little Morenos and their nurses and servants brought me. We just filled the car nicely. And oh! we did have such a good time! Did you ever go anywhere in a Pullman car, cousin Mangan? If you didn't, you don't know at all how nice it is. Not a bit like the horrid *diligencia*, you know. And we did have such fun! I had my dear Pablo— he's the parrot, you know; and the Señora Moreno had a—I don't know what the English name is: it's a bird that whistles and sings wonderfully; and little Joséfita had a yellow kitten; and at Chihuahua each of the seven boys bought a dear little dog. When Pablo was screaming, and the bird was whistling, and the kitten was fighting with all the little dogs at once, really, we could not hear ourselves speak. It was so funny that we were laughing every bit of the time.

"And, cousin Mangan, Señor Moreno wanted to come here with me and give me into your hands. But I wouldn't let him. They all stopped at a little hotel quite near here, where Spanish is spoken—for Señor Moreno does not speak a word of English, and I have done all the talking for him ever since we left Paso del Norte; you have no idea what nice things the conductors and people have said to me about my English— and I begged Señor Moreno to let me come in the carriage by myself. I wanted to surprise you, you see. *Have* I surprised you, cousin Mangan ? Tell me truly, *have* I !"

And Mr. Mangan Brown answered, in a tone that Miss Carmine, possibly, thought unnecessarily serious : " Yes, my dear, *I*

believe that I may say with perfect truth—
you have ! "

NATURALLY, so quiet a household as was
this of Mr. Mangan Brown's was a good deal
upset by having interjected into it such a
whirlwind of a young woman as was this
Miss Violet Carmine. The household was
quieter than ever, of course, now that Miss
Caledonia and Verona were married off.
The wedding, by the way, was a prodigious
success. Mr. Mangan Brown gave away the
brides, successively, with a defiant one-down-
and-t'-other-come-on air that was tremendously effective ; and young Orpiment went
through with the ceremony gallantly ; and
Mr. Gamboge, who was badly scared, most
certainly would have said " Under these circumstances Mr. Orpiment would have said
' I will,' " if Miss Caledonia, being on the
lookout for precisely this emergency, had
not pinched him ; and Miss Caledonia looked
so young and so pretty in her gray silk and
new back hair that nobody ever would have

thought her a day over forty; and Verona just looked like the lovable, dignified angel that she was.

But while Miss Carmine found no difficulty in filling with her belongings the two rooms lately occupied by Miss Caledonia and Verona, it cannot be said that she herself filled precisely the place in the household which had been filled by these its departed members. Mr. Mangan tried loyally to make the best of his Mexican kinswoman, but even he found her at times—as he deprecatingly admitted to Rose—a little wearing. He tried to convince himself that Pablo's violent remarks, in the Spanish tongue, at atrocious hours of the morning, did not disturb him; he tried to believe that he admired the spirited playfulness of the seven little Moreno boys when they came to visit their countrywoman, and with their countrywoman and their seven Chihuahua dogs raced in and out of the parlor windows and up and down the veranda steps and all over the flower beds in the front garden; and he tried to think that his kinswoman's habitual tendency toward the violent and the unexpected did not annoy him. But it is certain that his efforts in these, and in various other, directions were not at all times successful. And yet when Violet was not doing something outrageous—which, to be sure, was not often—she was such a frank, affectionate body that not to love her was quite impossible.

"It's not herself, it's her extraordinary education that's at fault, Van," Mr. Mangan declared in extenuation of her expedition with Rowney Mauve and without a chaperon to Coney Island. "She's a good little thing, but what with her queer life on her father's *hacienda*, and the queer doctrines which her father and mother have got into her head, it's no wonder that her notions of propriety are a little eccentric."

Being lectured about her Coney Island trip, Violet manifested only astonishment. "Why, cousin Mangan, I thought that here in America girls could do just as they pleased. That's what mamma has always told me.

I'm sure that *she* did what she pleased when she was a girl.   And mamma was very carefully brought up and moved in very elegant society, you know.   Grandpapa, you know, sold outfits at Fort Leavenworth to people going across the Plains ; and he did a splendid business, too, in the Santa Fé trade. That was before the railroad, of course. Were you ever out along the Santa Fé trail before the Atchison road was built, cousin Mangan ?   It was a splendid trip to make. Mamma came out that way to Santa Fé in 1860 with grandpapa.   They had a lovely time ; just as full of excitement as possible. They had one fight with Indians before they were fifty miles out from Council Grove, and another just as they struck off from the Arkansas, and another at the crossing of the Cimarron ; and they were caught in a tremendous snow-storm in the Raton Mountains ; and in fording the Pecos they lost a wagon and its team of six mules—and grandpapa was so angry with the head teamster for his carelessness, that he just picked him up bodily and chucked him in after the mules, and then shot at him when he tried to swim ashore ; and mamma used to say in her droll way that they never knew whether that teamster died of drowning or shooting.

" It was in Santa Fé, you know, that papa met mamma and fell in love with her. It was very romantic. Mamma had made a bet with one of the officers of the garrison that she could ride a mustang that never had been broken; and it ran away with her—which mamma did not mind a bit, of course —and just as she was waving her handkerchief to the men to show that she was win-. ning the bet she found that the mustang was heading right for the edge of the bluff—she was riding on the *mesa* close by old Fort Marcy—and as she couldn't turn it she knew that they both were going to have their necks broken. And then papa, who was with the officers, saw her danger and galloped up just in time to lift her right out of the saddle while both horses were running as hard as ever they could run ; and papa managed to turn his horse on the very edge of the bluff, and the mustang went over the bluff and was done for.   Of course, after he had saved her life this way, and after he had fought a duel with the officer that mamma bet with, because he said that mamma had not won the bet after all, mamma had to marry him.   They had a lovely wedding in the old church of San Miguel, and all the officers were there—the officer whom papa wounded was ever so nice about it and came on crutches—and all the best people of the town were there too, and they had a splendid banquet at the Fonda afterward.   You see, there was no trouble about their being married, for mamma was born in the Church. Her mother's folks, the Smalts, were German Catholics, and, of course, her father was a Catholic too, for he was Don Patricio O'Jara, you know.   The O'Jaras are a very noble family, cousin Mangan ; some of them once were kings, mamma says.

"And because she belonged to such a grand family, and because grandpapa was so

rich, mamma moved in the very highest cir-
cles of Leavenworth society, you see ; and I
am sure that she went around with young
gentlemen just as much as she pleased, for
she has told me so, often.   So what was the
harm in my going to Coney Island with Mr.
Mauve, cousin Mangan ?   And we did have
such a lovely time !   Now you aren't angry
with me, are you ?   Then kiss me, and say
you're not—so.   That's a dear.   And now
we never will say another word about the
horrid place again."

Rowney Mauve, of course, knew that the
Coney Island expedition was all wrong ; and
he had the grace to profess to be sorry when
Van took it on himself to give him a lecture
about it.   Rowney was a rather weak vessel,
morally—as he admitted with a charming
frankness when anybody spoke to him on the
subject—and he never made any very perceptible effort to strengthen himself.   It
wasn't his ambition to be a whited sepulchre,
he would say, with an air of cheerful resigna-
tion that, in its way, was quite irresistible.

But, after all, he was not half a bad fellow at bottom.   His besetting sin was his laziness. Unless he had some scheme of pleasure on hand—when he would rouse up and work like a beaver—he was about as lazy as a man well could be.   Had he ever buckled down to work, there was the making of a first-rate painter in him.   Two or three landscapes which, by some extraordinary chance, he had finished, had been quite the talk of the town and had sold promptly. But there he stopped.

"Of course, old man, I know that I could sell a lot of pictures if I painted them," he would say when Van upbraided him for his laziness.   "But what's the good of it? I don't need the money.   I've got more now than I know what to do with."   And then he would add, in the high moral key and with the twinkle in the corners of his blue eyes that always came there in nice appreciation of his own humbug, "And I don't think it's right, Van, you know, to sell my pictures and so take the bread out of the mouths of the men who need it.   No, I pre fer to be as that cheerful old father-in-law of yours once said to me when he sent his ' Baby's First Steps ' to the Young Genius's exhibition, and the Young Geniuses cracked it right back at him—' a willing sacrifice for Art's great sake to other men's success.' That's a noble sentiment, isn't it ? And now, what do you say to joining me on board the yacht to-morrow and sliding down to Saint Augustine for a week or two ? There are some types among those stunning Minorcan girls down there that will make you a bigger swell in art than ever if you will catch them in time for the spring exhibition." The fact of the matter was that Rowney Mauve, in the matter of laziness, simply was incorrigible.

In connection with Miss Carmine, how-ever, not the least trace of Rowney's lazi-ness was perceptible. In her service he was all energy. Why, he even went so far as to finish one of his numerous unfinished pict-ures because, when Van and Rose brought her to his studio one day, she took a fancy to it and told him that she would like to see it completed! Among the people who knew him this outburst of zealous labor was regarded as being little short of miraculous; and Rowney, who was rather given to contemplative consideration of his own actions, could not help at first feeling that way about it himself. As the result of careful self-analysis, however, he came to the conclusion that his sudden access of energy was not the result of a miracle, but of love!

Being really in love was a new experience for Rowney, and he did not quite understand it. At one time or another he had been spoons on lots of girls; but being spoons and being genuinely in love, as he now perceived, were conditions of the heart which have no relation to each other whatever. Looking at his case critically, he was satisfied that his decline and fall had begun on that October day, now four months past, when he and Miss Carmine had defied the proprieties by going down together to Coney Island. They had seen the races, which Violet enjoyed immensely, and had had a capital little lunch; and after the lunch they had taken a long walk on the deserted beach toward Far Rockaway. Rowney knew all the while, of course, that they hadn't any business whatever to be off alone on a cruise of this nature; and his knowledge, I am sorry to say, made him regard the cruise in the light of a lark of quite exceptional jollity. Violet, not having the faintest suspicion that she was anything less than a model of American decorum, simply was in raptures. With a delightful frankness she repeatedly told Rowney what a good time she was having; and how like it was to the good times that her mother, the scion of the royal house of O'Jara, used to have in company with the young Chesterfields of Fort Leavenworth society.

Altogether, it had been an original sort of an experience for Rowney; and for this easy-going young gentleman original experiences had an exceeding great charm. Looking back, therefore, in the light of subsequent events, upon that particular day, he decided that it was the Coney Island expedition that had sapped the foundations of his previously well-fortified heart. Anyhow, without regard to when it began, he felt satisfied in his own mind that he was in love now, right over head and ears.

Roberson, whose studio was just across the passage, happened to drop in upon him at the very moment that he had arrived at this, to him, astonishing conclusion. Roberson was not a very promising sort of a specimen of a confidant, but Rowney was so full of his discovery that before he could check himself he had blurted out: " Old man, I've been and gone and done it! I'm in love!"

"No! Are you though, really?" said Roberson, in his funny little mincing way. "Why, that's very interesting. And who are you in love with?"

By this time Rowney had perceived the absurdity, not to say the stupidity, of taking Roberson into his confidence. So he laughed and answered:

"With my own laziness, of course. I've

been thinking what a precious ass I have been making of myself in working over this confounded picture. Now that it's finished, I don't know what to do with it, and I've wasted a solid month that I might have devoted to scientific loafing. And it's because I see my folly and am determined to be wise again that I've fallen in love with my own laziness once more."

"Oh!" said Roberson, in a tone of disappointment, "I thought that you were in earnest; and I was ever so glad, for I really am in love, Rowney, in love awfully! And—and I thought that if you were in love too, you'd like to hear about it. Wouldn't you like to hear about it anyway?"

"Of course I would, old man. Just wait till I fill my pipe; I can be more sympathetic over a pipe, you know. Now crack away," Rowney continued, as he settled himself comfortably in a big chair and pulled hard at his pipe to give it a good start. "Now crack away, my stricken deer. Though the herd all forsake thee, thy home is still here, you know. Rest on this bosom and tell your tale of sorrow. Are you very hard hit, Roberson?"

"Oh! I am, indeed, I am," groaned Roberson. "You see, its—its this queer Mexican girl who is staying with the Browns——"

"The dickens it is!" exclaimed Rowney, suddenly sitting bolt upright in his chair, and glaring at Roberson through the smoke as though he wanted to glare his head off.

"Don't, please don't look at me like that, Mauve. Surely there's no reason why you should be angry with me."

"N—no," answered Rowney slowly, "I don't think there is." And then, as he sank back in the chair, and his ferocious expression gave place to a quiet grin, he added briskly: "No, I'm sure there's not. I was surprised, that's all. I always look like that when I'm a good deal surprised."

"Well, I must say I'm glad I don't surprise you often. You have no idea how savage you looked, old fellow. I'm not easily frightened, you know," and the little man put on a look of inoffensive defiance as he spoke that gave him something the air of a valorously-disposed lamb; "but I do assure you that the way you looked at me gave me quite a turn. Just let me know, won't you, when you feel yourself beginning to be surprised the next time, so that I may be prepared for it?"

"I'll do better than that, Roberson; I'll promise not to let you surprise me. And now go ahead with the love story, old man; I'm quite ashamed of myself for having interrupted you so rudely."

"There isn't any more of it to tell," said Roberson, dolefully. "I wish there was."

"Nonsense, man! Why, that isn't any love story at all. There *must* be more of it. What have you said to her? What has she said to you?"

"Nothing," answered Roberson, dismally. "That's just it, you see. That's what makes me so low in my mind over it. I haven't said anything, and she hasn't said anything.

If either of us had said anything I'd know better where I was. But neither of us has spoken, and so I don't know where I am at all—not the least bit in the world." Roberson hid his face in his hands and groaned.

Presently he went on again: "I have made efforts to speak, Rowney; I've made repeated efforts—but, somehow, they've none of them come to anything. Indeed, I've never had but one fair chance, for every time, just as I've got to the point when I was ready to say something, something that really would have a meaning to it, you know, something has happened to stop me."

"And what stopped you that one time when something didn't happen to stop you?"

"You mustn't think me weak, Rowney, but—but the truth is that I was so dreadfully upset that what I wanted to say wouldn't come at all. We were sitting on the veranda, the moon was shining, and all the rest were inside listening to Mrs. Orpiment singing. I couldn't have had a better chance, you see."

" I should think not ! " growled Rowney.

" But the more I tried the more the right words wouldn't come. And what do you suppose I ended by asking her ? "

" If she didn't think you were an infernal idiot. And of course she said yes."

" Don't be hard on me, Mauve. You've no idea what a trying situation it was. No, what I ended by asking her was, what was the food most commonly eaten in Mexico. I didn't say it in just a commonplace way, you know. I threw a great deal of feeling into my voice, and I looked at her beseech-ingly. And—and I think, old fellow, that she knew that my words meant more than they expressed, for there was a strange tremor in her own voice as she answered, ' tortillas and frijoles ; ' and as soon as she had uttered those brief words she got up and rushed into the parlor, as though something were after her. This was a very extraordi-nary thing for her to do, and it shows to my mind that she did not dare to trust herself with me for a moment longer. And I am the more confirmed in this opinion by the fact that when I followed her, in a minute or two, for at first I was too much surprised by her sudden departure to stir, I found her leaning upon Mrs. Brown's shoulder in hysterics—laughing and crying all at once, I solemnly assure you. Don't you think there's hope for me in all this, Rowney? Don't you think that her saying ' tortillas and frijoles ' in that strange, tremulous tone, and then having hysterics after it, meant more than I could understand at the time ? "

" Yes," answered Rowney, decidedly, " I think it did. To be quite frank with you, Roberson, I don't think that you fully understand just what she meant even yet."

" Oh, thank you, thank you, Mauve. You don't know how much good you are doing me by your kind, encouraging words."

Rowney's conscience did prick him a little when Roberson said this—but only a little, for his resentment of what he styled in his own mind Roberson's confounded impudence in venturing to make love to Violet, was too keen for him to give the unlucky little man mercy in the least degree.

For a while there was silence. Mauve pulled away steadily at his pipe, and Roberson stared gloomily into vacancy and gently wrung his hands. At last he spoke :

" Rowney, do you believe that there is anything in—in spiritualism ?"

" There's dollars in it, if you only can make it go. Why ? Are you thinking of taking it up as a profession ? It's rather a shady profession, of course ; but you ought to make more out of it than you do out of your still-life stuff. The properties wouldn't take much capital to start with. Two rooms in an out-of-the-way street—Grove Street would do nicely ; some curtains, and a table ; that's all you'd need to begin with. If things went along well, and you found that there was a paying demand for materializations, then you'd have to get some costumes. And what awfully good fun it will be ! " Rowney continued, as he warmed up to the subject. " Do you know, I've a great mind to go in with you. It will be no end of a lark."

"Oh, you don't understand me at all, Mauve. I don't want to be a medium. What I mean is, do you believe in the reality of spiritual manifestations?"

Rowney was about to say "spiritual fiddle-sticks," but checked himself, and answered diplomatically: "Well, you see, I haven't much experience in that line, and so my opinion isn't especially valuable. Have you ever tackled the spirits yourself, Roberson?"

"Ye-es," answered Roberson, hesitatingly, "I have."

"And what sort of a time did you have with them?"

"Well—but you won't laugh at me, will you, Mauve? I'm really in earnest, you know, and if you only want to make a joke of it, I won't go on."

"Don't you see how serious I am?"

"Well, some of the spirits did tell me very wonderful things. Do you remember that picture that I painted a year ago last winter—peas, and asparagus, and Bermuda potatoes, and strawberries, grouped around a shad—that I called ' The First Breath of Spring ?' I don't think that you can have forgotten it, for it was a noble work. Well, the spirit of Jan Weenix told me to paint that picture, and promised me that it would bring me fortune and fame."

" Why, I saw it in your studio only yesterday, with a lot of other stuff piled up in a corner. Not much fame or fortune there, apparently. If that's the sort of game that the spirits come on you, I should say that they lie like Ananias and Sapphira."

" Hush ! don't speak that way, please. We never know what Form hovers near." (Roberson said this so earnestly that, involuntarily, Rowney glanced over his shoulder.) " It is true that the promise made by the spirit of Jan Weenix has not yet been fulfilled ; but, you know, there's no telling at what moment it will be. Every time that I hear a strange step on the stairs,

I say to myself: 'He comes! The Purchaser comes—and with him come Fortune
and Fame!' And though I'm bound to
admit I haven't seen the least sign of him
yet, that only assures me that I have so
much the less time to wait for his coming.

"Yes, I believe in the spirits thoroughly,
Mauve. Every action of my life, for years
past, has been guided by them. And I
believe that it is because I have not their
guidance in this great matter of my love
that I am going all wrong."

"What's the reason they won't guide you
now? Have you had a row with 'em?"

"I do wish that you wouldn't speak in
that irreverent way. No, the trouble is that
the medium whom I have been in the habit
of consulting for years has—has gone away.
In point of fact"—Roberson blushed a little,
" he has been arrested for swindling. It is a
great outrage, of course, and I am desperately sorry for him. But I am more sorry
for myself. You see, getting a new medium
is a very difficult matter. It is not only that

he must be a good medium intrinsically, but he must possess a nature that easily becomes *en rapport* with mine. When I began this conversation, it was in the faint hope that you also might be a believer and might be able to help me in my quest ; but I see now that this hope has no foundation. I must search on, alone—and until I find what I require I shall toss aimlessly upon the ocean of life like a rudderless ship in a storm. Don't think me ungrateful, old man, because I am so melancholy. Your sympathy has cheered me up ever so much. Indeed, I haven't been so light-hearted since I don't know when "—and with tears in his eyes and sorrow stamped upon every line of his face Roberson gently minced his way out of the room.

"I say, Roberson !" Rowney called after him. "I've a notion that I know a medium who is just the very card you want. I'll look him up, and if he's what I think he is, I'll pass him along to you."

"Oh, thank you, thank you very much,

Mauve," said Roberson, putting his head in at the door again. " It's ever so good of you to think of taking this trouble on my account. But if you will find me a new medium, a good one, you know, that I can trust implicitly, you really will make a new man of me." And uttering these hopeful words Roberson closed the door.

For an hour or more Rowney Mauve continued to sit and smoke in the big chair. During this period he grinned frequently, and once he laughed aloud. When at last he stood up and knocked the ashes from his third pipe, it was with the satisfied air of a man who has formulated an Idea.

At the outset of this narrative the fact has been mentioned that Violet Carmine was a pickle. The additional fact may be appropriately mentioned here that a residence of five months in the stimulating atmosphere of New York had not by any means tended to make her less picklesome. Except in the case of Mr. Mangan Brown, who stood by her loyally, she was the despair of the Eleventh Street household ; and she was not favorably commented upon abroad. After that dinner at the Gamboges—when Violet flirted so outrageously with young Orpiment that even Verona's placid spirit was ruffled—Mrs. Gamboge said to Mr. Gamboge, in the privacy of their own chamber, that she was very sure that this wild Mexican-Irish girl would bring all their gray hairs down in sorrow to the grave. Mr. Gamboge, who had a rather soft spot in his heart for Violet, and to whom the mystery of Miss Caledonia's back hair was a mystery no longer, glanced shrewdly at the toilet-table, grinned in a manner that was highly exasperating, and made no reply. Mr. Gamboge regretted his adoption of this line of rejoinder ; but Mrs. Gamboge—having suffered peace to be restored when she found herself in possession of the Indian shawl for which her heart had panted all winter long—inclined to the opinion that brutality was not without its compensating advantages, after all.

And being a pickle, Violet threw herself, heart and soul, into the part assigned to her by Rowney Mauve in the realization of his Idea.

" It's delightful, Rowney ! "—" Mamma always used to call her gentlemen friends at Fort Leavenworth by their first names, cousin Mangan. I am sure that you might let me do what mamma did," Miss Carmine had observed with dignity, when Mr. Mangan had suggested to her one day that this somewhat unceremonious mode of address might be modified advantageously.

" It's delightful, Rowney ! Really, I didn't think that you had the wit to think of doing anything so funny. Of course, I'll keep as dark about it as possible. If that sweet little Rose were to get wind of it, I believe she'd faint ; and funny little old cousin Caledonia would have a fit ; and Van would be seriously horrified and disagreeable. And even cousin Mangan, who is the dearest dear that ever was, wouldn't like it ; and he'd end by coaxing me out of it, I'm sure.

And I don't want to be coaxed out of it,
Rowney, for it will be the best bit of fun
that I ever had anything to do with. But
I'll have to have somebody along, you
know. And I'll tell you who it will be:
that nice Rose d'Antimoine! She's just as
bad as they all say I am. I don't think
that I'm very bad, Rowney; do you? Only
she's sly, and knows how to pretend that
she isn't. May I tell her about it, and ask
her to take a hand? You'd better say yes,
for unless she comes in I'll stay out, you
know."

Rowney, who was acquainted only with
society young American women, and to
whom the natural young American woman's
instinct of self-preservation, that is most
shrewdly manifested in her determination
always to have one of her sex with her
in her escapades, was unknown, was rather
staggered by this proposition, and was disposed to raise objections to it. But Miss
Carmine gave him to understand in short
order that his objections could not be enter-

tained for a moment. He would do what she wanted, she told him decidedly, or he would not do anything at all. And Rowney, not altogether unwillingly, for he did not want to get Violet into a scrape, gave in. Therefore the aid of Madame d'Antimoine was sought, and was given with effusion; for marriage had not tended to make her take a view of life much more serious than that which she had entertained when her scandalous flirtation with the "Marquis" had driven poor Jaune almost to extremities. So these three lively young people laid their reprehensible heads together, and if Roberson's ears did not burn, it was no fault of theirs.

It was the morning after this conference that Rowney Mauve dropped in upon Roberson in his studio.

"Oh! I'm ever so glad to see you, Mauve," said Roberson. "I was just wishing for somebody to come in to tell me about this thing. I'm not satisfied with it exactly, and yet I don't know what there is wrong about it either. I must explain though what I'm driving at. I call it 'The Real and the Ideal,' though I've been thinking that possibly 'High Life and Low Life' will be better. On this side, you see, I have a pile of turnips and a cabbage and a mackerel, and on this side a vase of roses and a glass globe with goldfish in it. The idea's capital—contrast and that sort of thing, you know. But somehow the picture don't seem to come together. I've changed the composition two or three times, but I don't seem to get what I want. I do wish that you'd give me your advice about it, what you honestly think, you know."

"To tell the truth, Roberson, the way you've got it now—the things all jumbled together in a heap like that—it looks a good deal like nine-pins after the first ball has cracked into 'em."

"No? does it though? Why, I do believe you're right, Mauve. I've been thinking myself that perhaps the composition was too scattery. And yet I think there's a good effect in the way that they rise gradually from this one turnip here on the left to the roses on the right. I can't paint out those roses again, they're too good—don't you think that they're better than Lambdin's? I do. But I might move the globe of goldfish over to the left, and then have the mackerel and the vegetables along in a row between it and the roses. How do you think that would do? I've got to do something in a hurry, for the mackerel is beginning to smell horribly. I hope you don't find it very bad. I put carbolic acid over it this morning. Oh dear! Mauve. I don't seem to be able to do anything in these days ; now—now," and Roberson's voice became lower and had a tone of awe in it, " that I no longer have a Guide, you know."

" That's just what I came to speak to you about, Roberson."

" Goodness gracious! Mauve, you don't mean to say that you have—that you have found a Medium?" exclaimed Roberson in great excitement, springing up from his chair and dropping his palette and mahlstick with a clatter.

" That is just what I do mean to say, old man ; but I wish that you wouldn't jump around so. It disturbs the atmosphere and stirs up the smell of the fish horribly!"

" Oh! I beg your pardon. Just wait a minute and I'll put some more carbolic acid on it. Now tell me about him. Is he really a good medium? Have you tested him ? Is he knocks, or voices, or a slate ? Is he—"

" He isn't ' he ' at all ; he's a she."

" A ' she ' ? "

" Yes, a woman medium, you know."

" Oh," said Roberson, doubtfully, and with less brightness in his face, " I've never tried a woman medium. Do you think they're apt to be as good as men ? "

" Not as a rule," Rowney answered, in the grave, careful tone of one who had given the subject a very thorough investigation and whose decision was final. " No, not as a rule ; but as an exception, yes. Dugald Stuart, in his admirable chapter on clairvoyance—spiritualism hadn't come up in his day, you know—says that 'the delicate, super-sensitive nerve-fibre of women renders them far more keenly acute to psychic influences than are men. It is for this reason that women, and women only, have given us trustworthy evidences of clairvoyant phenomena.' The eminent Professor Crookes, during his recent exhaustive and most fruitful experiments upon the element to which he has given the name of psychic force, has arrived at a conclusion which substantially is identical with that arrived at by the great Scotch philosopher. He says, clearly and positively, ' while the majority of my experiments with women have been failures, it is a notable fact that of all my experiments the only ones which have been completely and entirely satisfactory have been those in which the operating force was a woman ; and from this fact I conclude that only in the exquisitely sensitive nervous structure of women can proper media for the most interesting, the most astonishing class of psychic phenomena be found.' Now what can you say in opposition to this positively expressed opinion of the great English scientist? Surely, Roberson, you will not have the temerity, not to say the downright impudence, to set up your opinion, based only on your own meagre experience, against that of this profound investigator ; against the dictum of the man who has invented the Radiometer ?"

Roberson was greatly astonished, as well as greatly impressed, by this eloquent and learned outburst—and he was a good deal puzzled, later, when his most diligent search through the works of the authors named failed to discover the passages, or anything at all like them, that Rowney had quoted.

" What a wonderful fellow you are, Mauve !" he said, admiringly. " I had no idea that you had gone into the matter in this serious way."

" Well, when I set out to know anything, I do like to know it pretty thoroughly," Rowney answered airily. " But I hope that what I've said has weakened your prejudice against women-mediums. A man of your strong intellect, Roberson, has no right to entertain a prejudice like that. Of course, though, if you don't believe in women-mediums, we will say no more about this one that I have found for you."

" Oh, please don't speak that way, Mauve. I see that I have been very foolish, and I want to meet this one very much, indeed. Who is she ? "

" She's a Theosoph."

" A what ? "

" A Theosoph—a member of that wonderful and mysterious Oriental Cult that Madame Blavatsky so ably has expounded. But, of course, you know all about Theosophism ? "

" I know about it in a general way, you know. It's something like—like animal magnetism, isn't it ? "

" Yes, it's something of that general nature." Rowney found that he was getting into rather deep water himself, and he floundered a little in getting out of it

"Yes, it's like animal magnetism in a general sort of way.   And having this magnetic basis, you see, of course, it affords a wonderfully perfect channel for communication with the spirit world."

"Of course," Roberson assented.

"And this particular medium," Rowney continued, speaking with confidence again, now that the awkward turn in the conversation was safely past, "is without exception the most extraordinary medium that even Theosophism has produced.   She does everything that ordinary mediums do, and some most astonishing things that they don't.   Of course you've seen materializations, Roberson ? "

"Oh, yes, repeatedly."

"But of people who were dead ? "

"Of course."

"Well, this Theosoph will show you, will actually show you materializations of the living."

"You don't say ! " said Roberson, greatly interested.

"It's a fact, I assure you. This has never been done before, and even she has been able to do it only recently—after twelve years of study among the oldest Pajamas of the Cult in India. It's wonderful! And what is more, she can materialize inanimate objects—can make things in distant places appear visibly before your eyes. Of course she can do the trance business, and knocks, and slate writing, and all that sort of thing, you might say, with one hand."

"Wonderful! wonderful!" exclaimed Roberson.

"Right you are, my boy. She is the most wonderful medium that the world, at least the Western World, has ever known. She is—she is what a Colorado newspaper person would call a regular daisy, and no mistake!"

"And when can I see her, and where? Oh, Mauve, my heart is beginning to brighten again. I'm sure that she will set me in the right way again about my pictures, and—and about Violet, you know."

It was with some difficulty that Rowney restrained his strong desire to box Roberson's ears for this free use of Miss Carmine's name. But he did restrain himself, and answered : "You shall see her this very night, and in my studio. She is here in New York only for a day or two—she starts for India again at the end of the week—and has no regular place for her séances, so I have arranged with her to come to my studio this evening at eight o'clock. Will that suit you ?"

"Yes, yes ; and thank you a thousand times, Mauve. I shall be grateful to you all my life for what you have done."

"Will you, though ? Don't be too sure about that," said Rowney with a queer smile. "Good-by till eight o'clock. Phew ! how that fish does smell ! "

EGYPTIAN darkness reigned in Rowney Mauve's studio when Roberson entered it at eight o'clock that evening. Roberson did not more than half like this gloom and mystery. Rowney, leading him to a seat, felt that he was trembling. " Has the Indian lady come yet ? " he asked in a shaky voice.

" The Theosoph ? Yes, here she is. Permit me to present to you, madame, an earnest seeker after truth."

" It is well," was answered in a deep voice that quavered as though with suppressed emotion. " What seeks this earnest seeker ? "

" Now, crack away and ask about the picture. You'd better begin with that, and take the other matter afterward," Rowney whispered.

" Mustn't I call up an advising spirit first ? That's the usual way of beginning a séance, you know."

" Oh, of course, that's what I meant you to do," Rowney answered, in some slight confusion.

" Is the spirit of Jan Weenix present ? " asked Roberson.

There was a regular volley of raps, and then the deep voice answered " He is ! "

("*It* is ; there is no sex in spirits," murmured Rowney, sotto voce.)

" I am ever so glad to meet you again," Roberson said, quite in the tone of one who greets an old friend after a long separation. " I'm dreadfully muddled about this new picture of mine, ' High Life and Low Life,' you know. Won't you please tell me what I must do to get it right ? "

" Behold it as the great Weenix himself has painted it ! " and the deep voice was deeper, and also shakier than ever.

" Now you will see one of the wonderful materializations that I told you about," Rowney whispered. " Only the most highly-gifted even of the Theosophs can do this sort of thing. Look ! "

In one corner of the room there appeared a soft, hazy glow, covering a space of about three feet square. The haze passed slowly away, and as the brightness increased, a picture became visible. It was Roberson's picture, sure enough, but the composition had been modified materially. The rosebush was in the centre; on one side of it was the glass globe, filled with the vegetables; on the other side was the mackerel, standing straight up on its tail, while the four goldfish, standing on their tails and touching fins, were circling around it in a waltz.

"Oh!" was all that Roberson could say on beholding this astonishing rearrangement of his work.

"Now, isn't that wonderful?" Rowney asked impressively.

"Ye—es, it certainly is," Roberson answered with hesitation. "At least it's very wonderful as a materialization; indeed, I never saw anything like it. But—but really, you know, Mauve, this arrangement of the picture is a most extraordinary one. Is it possible, do you think, that a malignant spirit has obtained control of the medium? You know that does happen sometimes."

"Like getting the wrong fellow at the telephone," suggested Rowney.

"Precisely," Roberson answered.

"And what do you do then? With the

telephone you ring for the exchange again and swear at them. But that wouldn't do with the spirits, I suppose."

"Of course not," said Roberson, a good deal horrified. "No, the proper thing to do when this happens is to drop all attempts to communicate with the spirit that has been called, and the effort of which to come has been frustrated, and to continue the séance with others less susceptible to malignant influences."

"With the Theosophs the custom differs a little. Being more potent than ordinary mediums, they usually insist upon the attendance of the spirit called. Still, it might be well in this case to adopt the plan that you mention. Suppose you go right ahead and demand a materialization of Miss Carmine, and then have things out with her."

"You don't mean to say that the medium can do that?"

"Indeed I do. Didn't I tell you that these Theosophs could materialize living people? You don't seem to understand,

Roberson, what a tremendous power is here at our command. But I'll manage it for you." And Rowney continued in a deep, solemn tone : "Madam, I conjure you to compel the visible presence of the spirit of Violet Carmine."

As Rowney ceased speaking, the materialized picture vanished, the hazy light disappeared, and profound darkness came again. Then the phenomenon of the gradual appearance of the light was repeated ; but this time they beheld behind the misty veil not Roberson's reconstructed picture, but the wraith of Violet herself. Oddly enough, the beautiful apparition seemed to be doing its best not to laugh.

Roberson was so overpowered by this astounding sight that he was speechless. It was monstrous, this awful power that could subject a living being to its sway, so far beyond anything that he ever had encountered in the course of his spiritual investigations, that a great fear seized him. Cold perspiration started upon his forehead, and his knees shook.

" Well, you goose, now that I'm here haven't you anything to say for yourself ? Can't you even ask me about what people eat in Mexico ? " Voice, tone, and manner were Violet's to the life. It was too much for Roberson. His demoralization was complete.

" Mauve ! Mauve ! for heaven's sake help me to get away ! This is no ordinary medium. It is the very Power of Evil that we have invoked ! "

" That's a pretty compliment to pay a lady, now isn't it ? " and the apparition spoke with a certain amount of sharpness. " As I didn't come here to be called bad names, I shall leave—and the next time that you have a chance to speak to me you'll be apt to know it, my lad ! " with these decisive words Miss Carmine's wraith faded away, and the misty light slowly vanished into darkness.

" Oh take me away ! take me away ! " moaned Roberson feebly. In his terror he had sunk down in a little heap of misery upon the floor.

"All right, old man. Just wait half a minute, though, until I speak a word to the Theosoph."

Roberson heard Rowney cross the room ; perceived a momentary gleam of light—such as might come when a curtain that conceals a lamp is quickly raised and quickly dropped again—and then came the sound of whispering. Roberson's fear was leaving him a lit-tle now ; but in the darkness, without Rowney to guide him, he did not dare to stir. Suddenly the whispering, becoming less guarded, was audible.

"You shan't ! Go away ! "

"I shall ! I can't help it ! You've no idea what a lovely ghost you made ! "

Then there was a sound of a scuffle, that ended in a crash—and there, seen in a blaze of light over the fallen screen, was Rowney Mauve in the very act of kissing Violet Carmine. The whole apparatus of the trick was disclosed. In the part of the screen that remained standing was the square hole where the picture had been visible ; and the gradual

coming and going of the light, and its misti-
ness, were accounted for by the dozen or so
of gauze curtains arranged to draw back one
by one. And there was the picture itself—
even more shocking when seen clearly than
when hidden by the misty veil. On the
outer side of the screen, where she could manage the curtains, stood Rose d'Antimoine.

As he sat there on the floor and perceived
by these several disclosures how careful the
preparations had been for making a fool of
him, and as he painfully realized how admir-
ably well he had been fooled, fear ceased to
hold possession of Roberson, and in its place
came spiteful rage.

"It's a nasty, mean trick that you have
played on me; and I'll get even with you for
it, see if I don't! You ought to be ashamed
of yourselves, every one of you; and I'll
make you ashamed, too, before I get through
with you."

"Oh, come now, old fellow, it was only a
joke you know. Don't be unreasonable
about it and raise a row."

"You may think it a joke, Mauve, to have these ladies here at your studio at night, and to go on in that scandalous way with Miss Carmine, but I don't think that either Mr. d'Antimoine or Mr. Brown will see anything much of a joke in it! Oh, you'll all repent this! I'll teach you to play tricks! I'll fix you, you mean things!" Roberson's voice, never a deep one, rose to a shrill treble as he delivered these threats, and in a perfect little whirl of fury he rushed out of the room.

The fact must be admitted that the three conspirators, being thus delivered over into the hands of their intended victim, were pretty badly crest-fallen. They knew that Roberson certainly had it in his power to make things exceedingly unpleasant for them ; and they knew, too, that he certainly intended to use his power to the very uttermost. Decidedly, the outlook was not a cheerful one. As they left the studio, and the wreck of their spirit-raising apparatus, they all three were in a chastened and melancholy frame of mind.

"THERE'S been a dreadful rumpus, Rowney," Violet said, when, as they had agreed, they met in the friendly shelter of Madame d'Antimoine's drawing-room the next afternoon. "That mean little Roberson has told everybody everything, and—and hot water's no name for it! Mr. and Mrs. d'Antimoine have had a regular squabble, though they've made things up now; and Rose has been crying till her lovely blue eyes are all swollen and ugly; and Van is in a perfect Apache rage; and Verona is dignifiedly disagreeable; and little Mrs. Gamboge got so excited and indignant that her back-hair all went crooked and nearly came off, and she had to go upstairs and fix it; and dear little Mr. Gamboge looks solemnly at me, and I heard him say as I came by the parlor-door: ' I am sure that Mr. Orpiment would not have hesitated to characterize such conduct as highly reprehensible.' And the wo-worst of all, Rowney," and Violet's voice broke and her eyes had tears in them, " is that cousin Mangan won't get comfortably angry and have it out with me, but is just miserable and mopes. All that he said to me was: ' Mr. Roberson has told me something that I have been very sorry to hear, my child,' and his voice didn't sound right, and I know that he wanted to cry. O Rowney, I'm the most wretched girl in the world!"

Rowney was feeling pretty low in his mind already, and this frank avowal of her misery by Violet made him feel a great deal lower; and he was cut the more keenly because neither by her words nor her manner did she imply that he was the cause of it—as he most certainly was.

"I am very, very sorry," he said.

"Yes, I'm sure you are, Rowney; and its ever so good of you, you dear boy. You see—you see," and Violet blushed delightfully, "what upsets them all so is your—your kissing me that way. Of course I know that you didn't mean anything by it, and I'm sure I don't see why they make such a fuss about it. Mamma has told me that several of her gentlemen friends at Fort Leavenworth used to kiss her whenever they got a chance, and that she always used to box their ears whenever they did it. Now, I wonder," Violet continued, struck by a happy thought, "I wonder if it's because I didn't box your ears that they all object to it so? Because if it is, you know, I might do it yet. Shall I?" and she looked at him half inquiringly, half with a most bewitching sauciness. The comfort of telling her troubles to so sympathetic a listener was having a very reviving effect upon her. She certainly did not look at all like the most wretched girl in the world now.

Rowney moved a little closer to her, they were sitting on the sofa, and took her hand in his. Then, rather shakily, he spoke: "Violet!"

She started. He never had called her Violet before. But she did not take away her hand.

"Violet!" Rowney's voice had not its usual mocking tone, but was quite grave and had a strange ring of tenderness in it. "My little girl, there's just one way for me to get you out of the scrape that I've got you into, and that's to marry you.   May I ? "

" O Rowney ! Do you mean to run away with me ? "

" Well, I hadn't exactly contemplated running away with you, I confess," said Rowney, grinning a little in spite of himself.

" Hadn't you, though ? " Violet answered, with a touch of disappointment. " Why, grandpapa ran away with grandmamma, and they had a lovely time. Colonel Smalt, that was grandmamma's father, you know, started right out after them with dogs and a shot-gun, and chased them for two whole days.   And at last they came to a river that they had to swim their horses across, and the Colonel, who was close behind them, swam after them.   And his horse was dead beat, and couldn't swim ; and the Colonel would have been drowned if grandpapa had not come back and rescued him.   And the Colonel insisted upon fighting grandpapa right there in the water, and he did cut him pretty badly ; and it was not until grandpapa held him under water until he was nearly drowned that the Colonel gave in. And then grandpapa carried him safely ashore ; and after that, of course, they were the best of friends. Wasn't it all delightful ? I've heard mamma say again and again, how much she was disappointed, because papa did not run away with her. So, don't you think, don't you really think, Rowney, that you'd better run away with me, dear ?"

"And have Mr. Mangan Brown, and Van, and Mr. Gamboge galloping after us, and swimming the Hudson, and peppering us with shot-guns ?"

"Yes! yes! Oh, *do* do it, Rowney. It would be such splendid fun, and would be so very romantic !"

"All right. If you really want to run away, I'd just as lief have things arranged that way as any other, and it certainly will save a lot of trouble. But don't count too

much on the shot-guns, for I don't think it
probable that Mr. Mangan Brown and Mr.
Gamboge will come out strong in that direction ; it isn't exactly their line.   And now'
let me have a kiss ; just one, to make it a
bargain, you know."

And Madame d'Antimoine coming in at
this moment assumed an air of stately be-
nevolence, and said : " Ah, my children, is
it thus ?   Let me then give to you the blessing, as is done by the good mamma in the
play ! "

MR. MANGAN BROWN did not adopt the
shot-gun policy.   Indeed, this policy was
rendered quite impracticable by the fact
that Rowney and Violet, immediately upon
accomplishing their marriage, did their running away on board of Rowney's yacht—a
mode of departure that Violet approved of
rapturously, because, as she said with much
truth, " it was so like eloping with a real
pirate."   But Mr. Mangan felt pretty dismal over it, and wrote a very apologetic

account of his stewardship to Señor Carmine. He tried to make the best of things,
of course, pointing out that in the matters of
family and fortune Rowney really was quite
a desirable son-in-law; but even after he
had made the best of it, he could not help
admitting to himself that the situation was
one that a prudent parent scarcely could be
expected very heartily to enjoy. And he
was most agreeably surprised, therefore, a
month or so later, when Señor Carmine's
letter escaped from the Mexican Post-Office,
and came to him laden with olive-branches,
instead of with the thunderbolts which he
had feared.

Violet's father was not angry; on the contrary, he seemed to be highly pleased with
the " excellent match " that his daughter had
made, and expressed his unqualified approval of the " spirited way " in which she
had made it. " She has done honor to herself, to her mother, and to the education
that she has received," Señor Carmine declared, " and we are very grateful to you for

giving her the opportunity that she has so well improved." The letter concluded with a most urgent invitation for Mr. Mangan to come down for six months or a year, and to bring with him Mr. and Mrs. Gamboge, Van and Rose, Verona and young Orpiment, and Monsieur and Madame d'Antimoine, with all of whom, this hospitable Mexican gentleman wrote, he had made a very pleasant acquaintance in his daughter's letters. And enclosed in this communication was a note, signed, Brígida O'Jara de Carmine, of which the theme was a breezy laudation of the love that defies conventionalities, and laughs at locksmiths, and is the true parent of romance !

"Well, since they take it this way," said Mr. Mangan Brown with a great sigh of relief as he laid down the letters, " I must say that I'm glad she's gone. At my time of life close association with such a—such a very volcanic young woman as Violet is, is rather overwhelming. It's like being the Czar of Russia and having the leading Nihilist right in the house with you. And it is a great comfort, just when I thought that everything was ending shockingly, to find that every-thing has ended pleasantly. For—except that Violet has left that confounded parrot behind her—everything *has* ended pleasantly, after all."

And only Roberson, among those who had enjoyed the rather mixed pleasure of Miss Carmine's acquaintance during her sojourn in New York, dissented from the optimistic view of the situation thus formulated by Mr. Mangan Brown. In this matter Roberson was not optimistic: he was a pessimist of the deepest dye. When he came to know what a boomerang his revenge had turned out to be he forswore both love and spirit-ualism and settled down to art with the stony calmness of despair. And it is a notable fact—though a fact not unparalleled —that the longer he painted the more abom-inably bad his still-lifes were !

A MEXICAN CAMPAIGN.

A MEXICAN CAMPAIGN.

I.

THE MOBILIZATION OF THE TROOPS.

MR. PEMBERTON LOGAN SMITH was a member of the Philadelphia Sketch Club; and by his associates in that eminently democratic organization it generally was conceded that if he had not been handicapped by the first two-thirds of his name, and if he had not been born constitutionally lazy, he probably would have made rather a shining light of himself as a landscape painter.

When this opinion was advanced in his presence, as it very frequently was, Pem usually laughed in his easy-going way and said that quite possibly it possessed some of the elements of truth. For Mr. Pemberton Logan Smith knew very well that he was constitutionally lazy, and he as frankly gloried in his double-barrelled Philadelphia name as he did in the fact that he was a Philadelphian to the backbone.

"You see, old man," he once explained to his New York friend, the eminent young figure-painter Vandyke Brown, "you New York people haven't much notion of birth, and family connection, and that sort of thing, anyway. There are, I believe," said Pem, airily, "a few good families in New York, but most of your so-called best people haven't the least notion in the world who their grandfathers were; or else—and this amounts to the same thing—they know so much about them that they want to keep them as dark as possible. All you care for over here is money. Now, that isn't our way at all. Of course we don't object to a man's having money; but the first thing we want him to have is birth. If he can show that his people came over with Penn—or before Penn, as mine did—and if he belongs to the Assembly, and is certain of his invitation to the Charity Ball, and a few things of that sort, we take him in; but if he hasn't this sort of a record—well, we think about it. Of course, now and then a fellow who has only money works his way into good society, provided he knows how to give a really good dinner and doesn't stint the terrapin. But that is the exception; the rule is the other way."

But while Brown and some of the Sketch Club men regretted that Pem did not buckle down to painting and accomplish some of the good work that he undoubtedly was capable of, Pem himself took the matter very easily. He had succeeded in developing enough energy to paint two or three pictures which deserved the praise that they received, and with this much accomplished he seemed to be quite contented to let his case rest.

In the Social Art Club, where the artistic element was infinitesimal, and where Pem's

social high qualifications were accepted at
their proper high value, he was regarded as
an artistic genius of a considerable magni-
tude. But this was only natural, for he
really knew something about pictures—instead of only partly knowing how to talk
about them.

And in both of his clubs, and pretty generally by his somewhat extensive personal acquaintance, Pem was set down—quite apart
from his qualifications as an artist—as a thoroughly good fellow. As a rule, a popular
verdict of this nature may be critically examined without being reversed. In certain quarters the fact was recognized that he had been
a little narrowed by the circumstances of his
birth and environment; but even in these
quarters it was admitted that there was something very pleasant about him—when he was
not shying cocoa-nuts from the heights of
his Philadelphia family tree. And finally,
the three or four people who really knew
him well, among whom was his friend Brown,
believed that there was an underlying strength

and earnestness in his character which would be aroused, and so fully as to become the governing force of his life, should any great joy or great calamity overtake him that would stir his nature to its depths.

A good-looking young fellow of five or six and twenty, with pleasant manners, plenty of money, a faculty for taking odd and amusing views of life, and having at least a spark of genius in his composition—a young fellow of this sort, I say, is not to be met with on every street corner; and when he is encountered, commonplace humanity, without precisely knowing why, rejoices in him; and uncommonplace humanity, knowing precisely why, rejoices in him too.

On the whole, therefore, it was very natural, when the Browns were casting about them for an eligible man to whom to offer the tenth section in the car which they had chartered for their Mexican expedition, that Mr. Pemberton Logan Smith should have been accorded the suffrages of the Mexican expeditioners with a flattering unanimity.

Quite as naturally, when this offer to join an exceptionally pleasant party in what promised to be an exceptionally pleasant international jaunt was made known to him, Mr. Pemberton Logan Smith promptly accepted it. And he was the more disposed to Mexican adventure because he had acquired a very satisfactory command of Spanish in the course of a recently passed delightful year in Spain.

The projector of the Mexican campaign was Mr. Mangan Brown. Through his leather connection in Boston, Mr. Brown had been induced to invest a considerable sum of money in what his Boston friends had described to him, at the time when the investment was made, as the highly philanthropic and very lucrative work of aiding in the railway development of Mexico. A fabulously rich country was waiting, they told him, to be aroused into active commercial life by the provision of adequate means of internal transportation; a sister Republic, they added, was pining to be bound to the great nation of the north by bonds of steel. Honor awaited the men who would accomplish this magnificent international work, while the substantial return for their philanthropy would be unlimited dividends in hard cash. It was a picturesque way of presenting a commercial enterprise, and Mr. Brown was moved by it. Pleased with the prospect of figuring to future generations in the guise of a continental benefactor, and not averse to receiving unlimited dividends, which would be all the more acceptable because they were so honorably earned, he listened to the voice of the Boston charmers—and drew his cheque in his customary liberal way.

His desire to go to Mexico, in part at least, grew out of his not altogether unnatural wish to find out why some of the promised generous dividends had not been declared. But aside from his financial interest in the sister republic, the erratic visitation of Miss Violet Carmine—now Mrs. Rowney Mauve —had inspired him with a strong curiosity to visit a country that was capable of producing so extraordinary a type of womanhood. And point had been given to this curiosity by the frequent warm invitations extended to him by his remote kinsman, Violet's father, to come to Mexico for a visit of indefinite length, accompanied by his family and a working majority of his friends. Hospitality of so boundless a type, Mr. Brown considered, in itself was a phase of sociology the study of which was very well worth a journey of three thousand miles.

And finally, with an eye to business, Mr. Brown believed that a visit to Mexico might be made to redound very materially to his interest in the matter of the direct importation of Mexican hides.

" The leather business is not what it used to be, Van," he remarked, somewhat gloomily, to his nephew, when this feature of the expedition was touched upon. " When I was a young man, serving my time with the late Mr. Orpiment's father, there were chances in leather that nowadays nobody would even dream of. I remember, in '46, our firm brought in two ship-loads of hides from Buenos Ayres, which were worth almost their weight in gold. They were made right up into shoes for Scott's army, you see. It always has rested a little heavily on my conscience, Van, that those hides were made up green that way. The shoes that they made of them must have worn out, I should say, in rather less than a week. But I wasn't really responsible for it, for I was only a boy in the counting - room; and even Mr. Orpiment wasn't responsible for what was done with the hides after they were sold. And our firm certainly made a pot of money out of the transaction. Of course, I can't hope now for anything as good as that was, no matter what I find in Mexico; but I am sure, all the same, that the Mexican leather market is worth looking into—and if all the Mexicans are like our cousin Carmine, they must be worth looking into also.

"By the way, I had a letter from Carmine to-day—he writes extraordinary English— in answer to mine telling him when we are

likely to get there ; and instead of being horrified at the prospect of having such a lot of
us bowling down on him, as I should be, I
know, he says that his only regret is that
there are not more of us coming. You'd think
that being called upon this way to entertain
twelve people, with only one in the whole
party whom he ever has laid eyes on, and,
besides Violet, only four—you and I, Verona
and your aunt Caledonia—who have the
smallest claim of blood relationship, would
upset even a Mexican's extended notions of
hospitality. But it doesn't a bit. He writes
in the friendliest way that he is looking forward with delight to having us all with him
for three or four months anyway, and urges
us to hurry down as quickly as possible.

" I confess, Van," Mr. Brown went on, self-
reproachfully, "that this whole-souled sort of
welcome makes me feel a little mean about
the half-hearted way in which we welcomed
Violet. And I really am ashamed to remember how thankful I was when she ran off with
your friend Rowney Mauve and got married.

To be sure, Violet wouldn't have been such a—such an abnormity, if it hadn't been for that confounded parrot. Thank heaven, she has consented to leave the parrot at home this time. I don't think that I could have gone myself if Violet had insisted, as at first she seemed disposed to, upon taking along that detestable bird. Parrots—parrots are awful things, Van!" And Mr. Brown obviously permitted his thoughts to wander back ruefully into a parrot-stricken past.

As to the party at large, it may be said—with the exception of Mr. Pemberton Logan Smith—to have organized itself. Van and Rose, Verona and young Orpiment, and Mr. and Mrs. Gamboge, were so closely bound by blood, marriage, and friendship to each other and to Mr. Mangan Brown, that they were as much a part of his plan as he was himself. Rowney Mauve and Violet, the son-in-law and the daughter of their prospective host in Mexico, naturally could not be left out. That Jaune d'Antimoine and his wife Rose (*née* Carthame) should come along was taken for granted by everybody. Indeed, these young French people were very close to the hearts of their American friends, and leaving them out of any plan as pleasant as this Mexican plan promised to be was not to be thought of.

Jaune, by the way, had made a great success in art since that day when Mr. Badger Brush had given him his first order. To be sure, as an animal-painter he could not hope to do work that would rank with Van's figure-painting; but he considered himself, and his wife considered him, as ranking far above young Orpiment. In this opinion, very naturally, neither young Orpiment nor Verona concurred. As to Verona, she entertained the profound conviction that landscape-painting was the very crown and glory of all forms of artistic expression; and she not less firmly believed that her husband was the highest expositor of that highest form of art. There was a little "Evening on the Hills," that young Orpiment had painted while they were on their wedding journey in

the Catskills, that Verona never permitted
him to sell, and that she was accustomed to
compare—to her husband's advantage—with
the finer work of Claude.   It will be observed
that some years of married life had not in the
least degree diminished — it could not well
have augmented—the strength of Verona's
wifely affection.

The party thus constituted comfortably
filled, with one section to spare, the Pullman
car that Mr. Mangan Brown, who cared a
great deal for comfort and very little for ex-
pense, had chartered for the expedition.
Mr. and Mrs. Gamboge, out of respect to
their superior age, and because of the need
for superior privacy involved in the commercial peculiarity of Mrs. Gamboge's back
hair, were accorded the cranny that the
Pullman people dignify with the name
of a "drawing-room;" and each of the
other members of the party had a section
apiece.

There was some little debate as to what
should be done with the spare section ; for

they all were agreed that another nice person
would be welcome; and equally agreed that
it would be a pity, in the interest of nice persons abstractly, to leave vacant a place that so
many people very gladly would fill.   The suggestion made by Rose to Van, somewhat tim-
idly, it must be confessed, that old Madder
should be invited, never came before the
house at all.   It was voted down promptly in
committee.   Van had a great deal of theoret-
ical devotion to his father-in-law, but he did
not see his way clear to this form of its practical expression.   With a wise diplomacy,
however, he refrained from making the matter personal.   After Rose was married old
Madder had taken a little apartment, and his
sister kept house for him.   It was here that
little Madder and Caledonia were to remain
while Rose and Van were in Mexico.   What
would become of the children, Brown asked,
if their grandfather went along?   And this,
of course, settled it.

A similar suggestion, similarly made in
private by his wife to Jaune d'Antimoine, in

regard to Madame Carthame, similarly received a firm though less skilful negative.

Old Madder probably never knew that his name had been mentioned in connection with the Mexican expedition at all ; and the diplomatic Madame d'Antimoine certainly did not permit her severe maternal relative to imagine for a moment that she had been weighed in her son-in-law's balance and found wanting. But after the party had started, old Madder certainly did say to Cremnitz White and Robert Lake, and one or two more of his especial cronies, that nothing under heaven could have induced him to accompany to Mexico, or to any other part of the world, a gang of painters that hadn't a single artist among them. And Madame Carthame likewise remarked, addressing her first-floor lodger, that she would not, under any circumstances, have permitted herself to associate with these her daughter's friends among the *nouveaux riches.*

It really looked as though the odd section in the Pullman would remain vacant—or that it would be utilized only as Rose suggested, as a cattery. Rose was very fond of cats, and to her mind the suggestion seemed to be a very reasonable one; for she wanted greatly to take her Persian cat, Beaux-yeux, along.

However, the feline member was not added to the party, for at this stage of proceedings Van put a large spoke in the wheel of his Philadelphia friend's fate by suggesting Mr. Pemberton Logan Smith as an eminently fit person to fill the vacancy. And so the organization of the friendly army of invasion was made complete.

II

THE ENGAGEMENT AT THE FRONTIER.

MRS. GAMBOGE approached the Mexican border with a heavy heart.

"Are the—the custom-house examinations *very* strict?" she asked of Mr. Gamboge, as they waited at the station in El Paso for the train that was to back across from the Mexican side of the river and hook on their car.

There was something in the tone of the lady's voice that caused her husband to look at her sharply, and to observe with some asperity: "You're not trying to smuggle anything, I hope?"

"N—no," responded Mrs. Gamboge, with a manifest hesitation. "But it—it's so horrid to have one's things all pulled to pieces, you know."

"You've got to make the best of it. You'd

have done better if you'd taken my advice
and not brought along such a lot of things
to pull," replied Mr. Gamboge, unfeelingly.
"What possible use you can have for two big
trunks on a trip of this sort, I'm sure I can't
imagine."

Mrs. Gamboge did not respond to this unkind remark. She retired at first into a pained
and dignified silence, and then into the privacy of the so-called drawing-room. A few
minutes later, when Mr. Gamboge—who was
a most amiable little round man—followed
her to this their joint apartment to make
amends for his mild severity, he found the
door locked; nor would Mrs. Gamboge for
some moments suffer him to enter. When
she emerged from her retreat there was an
expression of anxiety upon her usually placid
face; and until the custom-house examina-
tion was ended—which was in a very few
minutes, for the customs officials were refreshingly perfunctory in their methods—it
was evident that there was a weight upon
her mind.

As the train moved away southward, from Paso del Norte, Mr. Gamboge went into the "drawing-room" for his cigar-case, and was startled as he entered the apartment by a little shriek of alarm.

"Oh! I thought I'd locked the door," said Mrs. Gamboge, speaking with some confusion and at the same time hastily throwing a shawl over a cage-like structure that was lying on the seat. "Do go out, dear. You can come back in a moment."

"Caledonia," said Mr. Gamboge, seriously, "I hope that you have not really been smuggling. Let me see what you have under that shawl."

"I haven't been smuggling. Indeed, I haven't—at least nothing that I haven't a perfect right to. Do go away—only for a moment, but do go away."

All this was so out of keeping with the character of his wife—who, excepting in regard to the purely conventional secret of the commercial genesis of her back hair, never had made even an approach toward having a secret from him—that Mr. Gambòge was seriously discomposed.

"Indeed, my dear, you must let me see what you are hiding," he said, at the same time making a step forward and extending his hand toward the shawl.

"Oh, don't! don't, I beg of you!" Mrs. Gamboge implored, fairly wringing her plump little white hands. "It's—it's only my—my bustle. I've been taking it off."

"A bustle!" replied Mr. Gamboge, with both scorn and indignation. "Bustles are absurdities and monstrosities, and you very well may be ashamed of having anything to do with them. But as you have, to my certain knowledge, abandoned yourself to this species of deformity for several years past, and never have even remotely hinted that you wanted to make a mystery of your folly, I am at a loss to understand why you want to make a mystery of it now. Come, my dear, you must let me see what you have hidden here. I don't want to hurt your feelings, Caledonia, but indeed I must look."

And speaking thus firmly, Mr. Gamboge gently disengaged himself from his wife's restraining arms and lifted the shawl.

" It *is* a bustle, sure enough," he said, with some confusion. " But what's this inside of it ? " he added, in a different tone, as he perceived in the interior of the structure a carefully tied up little package of some apparently soft substance. Mrs. Gamboge made no reply. She was seated upon the sofa, gently sobbing.

" Why, Caledonia," cried Mr. Gamboge, in astonishment, as he unwrapped the parcel, " it's your back hair! And yet you have your hair on, just as usual. I—I am very sorry, Caledonia," he went on humbly, being overcome by the conviction that he had contrived at one and the same time to make a fool and a brute of himself. " Indeed, indeed, dear, I hadn't the least notion in the world what it was; I hadn't, upon my word. Will you—will you forgive me, Caledonia ? " Mr. Gamboge seated himself on the little sofa, placed his arm about his wife's plump waist, and gently drew her toward him.   He was very contrite.

Mrs. Gamboge, however, resisted his advances. "Go away," she said, between her sobs. "Go away! After all these years that you have been so good to me, I never thought you would do a thing like this. Now go and smoke your cigar. Of course, after a while I shall get over it, but you had better leave me now."

Mr. Gamboge, however, being truly penitent, was not to be thus repulsed. "I have been very rude," he said, "and, without meaning to be, very unkind. But I beg of you, Caledonia, to forgive me. You know how I love you, and you know that I would love you just as much if you were absolutely bald—which you are not, nor anything like it," Mr. Gamboge hastened to add, perceiving that the expression of his affection in these terms was unfortunate. "Your front hair is quite thick, positively thick, and that is the important place to have hair, after all." He spoke with more assurance, feeling that he was getting upon firmer ground. "So won't you try to forgive me, Caledonia? won't you try, dear?"

"Will you solemnly, solemnly promise," asked Mrs. Gamboge, still sobbing gently, but nestling her head a little closer on his shoulder as she spoke, "never to say a word about what has happened? I know that you won't speak about it to anybody else; but will you promise, on your sacred word of honor, never to speak about it again to me?"

Mr. Gamboge gave the desired pledge, and so peace was restored.

"I was so—so afraid that the custom-house man might find it, you see," Mrs. Gamboge explained a little later, as she still sat, with her husband's arm around her, on the sofa. "I wouldn't perhaps have minded the custom man," she continued, "nor even Verona, and not much Rose; but I couldn't bear the thought that that French young woman, Mrs. d'Antimoine, you know, should see it, for I know how Violet and she would have laughed."

And then she added, " It's—it's my spare hair, you know.   Don't you think that I did right to bring my spare hair along, dear ? "

Mr. Gamboge kissed her, and said that he thought she did.

III.

THE PARLEY UNDER FALSE COLORS.

THAT Mrs. Gamboge was a trifle melancholy during the day following her entry into Mexico cannot be denied; but her gloom was of a gentle, unobtrusive sort, and by no means affected the general high spirits of the party at large.

Violet Mauve, to be sure, was disposed to consider herself personally injured by her arrival at El Paso without having had the opportunity to enjoy the enlivening experience of a train robbery in Texas. Her earnest desire had been to come down to Vera Cruz in Rowney's yacht and to join the expedition in the City of Mexico; for she was convinced that Lafitte still sailed the Gulf, and it was the highest ambition of her life to be captured by a real pirate. Rowney's diplomatic suggestion that their train was pretty certain to be held up and robbed by Texan desperadoes alone had reconciled her to making the journey by rail; and as this pleasant possibility had not been realized, she felt herself to be a person whose rights as a lover of spirited adventure had been trampled upon.

"Don't you think that Rowney has treated me very badly, Mr. Smith?" she asked, with a good deal of indignation, when the safe arrival of the party in El Paso had made further chances for encounters with desperadoes impossible. "He as good as promised me that we should have a train robbery—and I always have so wanted to be in one—and for all that we have had in the way of adventure, excepting the horrible risks of our lives at the railway restaurants, we might as well have been spending our time riding backward and forward between Philadelphia and New York. Oh, how I wish now I'd insisted upon coming down in the yacht! Meeting a pirate in a long black schooner with a black flag and a skull and crossbones, and a desperately wicked crew, would have been so delightful! Don't you think so? And don't you think I have been very badly used indeed?"

"Well, in the matter of train robbers and pirates, Mrs. Mauve, I can't say that I have had enough personal experience to justify me in venturing on a very positive opinion, though I've no doubt they are great fun, just as you say. But as a Philadelphian I do know about eating "—Pem spoke with much feeling—" and I must say that on that score I think that you and all the rest of us have been treated abominably. It is not so much that the food is so wretched at these railway places, you know—for at some of them it really wasn't; but it's this horrible fashion the railway people have of treating their passengers as though they were locomotives—things that food and drink can be shovelled into and pumped into at the end of a section with a rush. But even a locomotive, I fancy," said Pem, gloomily, " would resent having all the coal and water that is to keep it going for the next six hours poked under and into its boiler in twenty minutes; and that's just what happens to the passengers, you know. I assure you, Mrs. Mauve, I haven't had the faintest approach to a comfortable meal since we left the Missouri River; and I know that I have made a long start toward ruining my digestion for the rest of my life.

"Of course the railway officials themselves must feed in this shocking way when they are travelling on their own trains. Now, I wonder," continued Pem, meditatively, " I wonder what a railway official is like? Do you suppose, Mrs. Mauve, that he has an inside, you know, like ordinary people; or that he is some form of highly specialized life from which environment, and selection, and that sort of thing has eliminated the digestive function altogether? I wish Darwin wasn't dead; I'd write and ask him."

Violet, whose knowledge of the doctrine of evolution was somewhat limited, was rather mystified by the turn that Pem had given to the conversation; but she accepted his suggestions in good part, and, seeing her way clear to answering a portion, at least, of his utterance, asked him, with a very fair show of sympathy, if his friend had been dead long.

Violet did not always quite understand what Pem was talking about; but she recognized the fact that he was a good deal of a piece, in his lazy, easy-going, queer ways, with her own husband, and she liked him accordingly. Indeed, the disposition of the entire party toward its Philadelphia member was of the friendliest sort. In speaking of his great-great-great-uncle, a distinguished Philadelphian of the past century, he had pleased and interested Mr. Mangan Brown by stating that this gentleman had been extensively engaged in the leather business. He had won the heart of Mrs. Gamboge by telling her—shortly after Mr. Gamboge had been giving one of his rather frequent funny little exhibitions of extreme vacillation of

purpose—that he greatly admired her husband because of his firmness of character.
He commended himself to Mr. Gamboge by
the thorough soundness of his rather old-
fashioned views upon dinners. The young
women of the party liked him because he had
the knack of doing and saying just the right
things at the right time; of never being in
the way, and of always being amusing. And
the young men liked him because he could
talk shop with them intelligently, and took
a lively interest—since the work was to be
done by somebody else—in their several artistic projects. In short, Pem found himself,
as he was in the habit of finding himself,
a general favorite.

"What a pity it is, Van," Rose observed
to her husband in the privacy of their chamber in the little Hotel Central in Aguas Calientes, "that your friend Mr. Smith does not
get married. I'm sure that he has the making of a very good husband. Of course he
wouldn't be a husband like you, dear, and
his wife couldn't expect to be as happy as I

am with you. But for just the ordinary sort of husband, I'm sure that he'd be much better than the average."

"He'd be obliged to you if he heard that somewhat qualified expression of approval."

"Yes, I suppose he would," Rose answered, in good faith. "But I think that he quite deserves it, for I believe that he would make a very good husband indeed. And do you know, Van," she continued, presently, "I think that there are a great many happy marriages in the world. I mean," she added, by way of expressing herself with absolute clearness, "marriages which are happy when they seem as if they certainly mustn't be."

Van looked a little puzzled.

"Now, you know those people we have noticed sitting opposite to us in the restaurant: the nice little Mexican woman, you know, and the German-looking man in black with the big nose?"

"The man like an underdone undertaker, who drinks beer, and who never opens his mouth except to give an order to the waiter?

You don't mean to say that that is a happy marriage, do you, Rose?"

"Indeed I do, and it was because I was thinking about those people that I said that a great many marriages which didn't seem happy really were.   She is a dear little woman, Van, and her life has been a regular romance.   She has had such heavy sorrows; and now everything has come right, and she is as happy as the day is long."

"Why, what do you know about her, child? Has she been telling you her life's history?"

"That's just what I'm coming to.   It is so interesting—just like a heroine in an old-fashioned novel.   This morning—while you were gone to look at those horrid dead dried-up monks, you know—I wanted Luciano to bring me some drinking-water.   I never shall get used to having chambermen instead of chambermaids, Van: I quite agree with Aunt Caledonia—I think it's horrid.   Well, I went out into the gallery and clapped my hands, and when Luciano came I said *agua*, and then I pointed to my mouth.   And he said something in Spanish, and pointed to the full water-bottle on the wash-stand. 'But I want fresh water, cool water,' I said. And Luciano did not understand at all, and only grinned at me. And just then that dear little Mrs. Heintzbach came out of her room and said in such nice English—she 's lived part of her life in California, she told me—that I needed a little help. And then she made Luciano understand what I wanted. So, of course, we got into talk then, and I invited her into our room, and she came, and she was so lady-like and so sweet that we got to be friends almost immediately."

"What! you made friends with that woman in that off-hand way!" Van seemed to be a good deal horrified, and he also seemed to be inclined to burst out laughing.

"I must say that I don't see what there was very remarkable about it," Rose responded, with some dignity. "She is a very charming woman, and not a 'that woman' sort of person at all. She belongs to very nice people, I'm sure."

"Yes, I'm sure she does, too—on her husband's side, especially," Van answered, with a chuckle. "Go on, Rosekin; I'm immensely interested."

"It's about her husband that I was going to tell you.   For all his silent, grave way, he is a delightful man, Van; as good and as kind as he can be. You see, when Mrs. Heintzbach was a young girl, a mere child of sixteen, her father and mother made her marry a horrid, rich Mexican, a friend of theirs, old enough to be her grandfather. He led her a perfectly shocking life. His jealousy was terrible! Why, he wouldn't even let her look out of a window on the street. He had all the front windows of their house bricked up, and never let her stir outside of the front door unless he went along with her. She told me with tears in her eyes that she knew that it was very wicked, but she couldn't help being so glad when he died that she wanted to dance! It was pretty horrible, when you come to think of it, to want to dance because your husband is dead; but, really, considering what sort of husband he was, I don't know that I can blame her."

"And then she married the gam — Mr. Heintzbach, I mean?"

"Yes—at least in a little while. She met him soon after her husband's death. And she had a chance to get to know him then, because she was a widow and it was all right for her to see him alone and talk with him comfortably. I never shall get used to the way women are treated here, Van; young girls kept perfect prisoners, and only married women and widows and very old maids given the least bit of freedom. It's shocking.

"Well, she saw a good deal of him, and she liked him from the first; and of course he liked her. And so, as soon as he decently could, he told her that he loved her; and the end of it was that in less than a year they were married. And he has made her such a good husband, Van! He is so loving and trustful and affectionate, so unlike her first husband, she says."

Brown was chuckling softly. "Did she say anything about her husband's business?" he asked.

"No, not directly. She spoke about his going every evening to the bank, I remember. But it can't be managed like our banks," Rose added, reflectively; "for our banks are not open in the evening, are they?"

Brown continued to chuckle. "Some of them are," he answered.

"And she spoke about his being kept out very late—till two or three o'clock in the morning. That isn't like our banks, I'm sure. And they are travelling almost constantly. She says that there is not a large city in Mexico that she has not visited with her husband. Her own home is in Guanajuato, and she has promised to give us letters of introduction to her people there; they must be very important people, from the way she spoke about them. Won't it be nice, Van, to have letters to the best people in Guanajuato? I thanked her ever so much; and I asked her to come and see us when she is in New York, and she said she certainly would. And early to-morrow morning, after she comes back from church—she is a very religious woman, and goes to church every morning, she says—we are to take a walk together in the little San Márcos park. She is very lonely in the early morning, she says, for her husband never gets up till ten o'clock. Aren't you pleased, Van, that all by myself I have made such a pleasant friend ?"

Brown was silent for a moment or two, and then startled his wife by exclaiming : "Well, by Jove! Rose, you have excelled yourself! You've picked up some queer friends at one time and another, but I never thought you'd ring in this way with the wife of a Dutch gambler !"

Rose sprang up with a little gasp. "Van ! What do you mean ?" she cried.

But her husband, instead of answering her, burst into such fits of laughter that he fairly held his sides. " Oh, what a commentary on all the tracts of the Tract Society," he said, at last, speaking with difficulty. " Upon my

word, I'll write a tract myself and call it,
'The Mexican Gambler's Wife; or, The
Happy Home'—the gambler a model of all
the domestic virtues, you know, and his wife
a shining example of simple, unostentatious
piety! O Rose! Rose! what a treasure-
house of unexpected delights you are!" And
Brown threw himself on one of the little
beds and laughed until the tears rolled from
his eyes.

"When you are *quite* done laughing, Van,"
said Rose with severity, but at the same time
with a decidedly frightened look, "will you
please tell me just what you mean? I know,
of course, that this good Mr. Heintzbach is
not a gambler; but he may be something—
something perhaps a little queer. Oh, have
I done anything *very* silly, Van?" And Rose
manifested symptoms of collapse, which were
intensified as her husband enfolded her in
his arms.

"It is as true as gospel, Rose," said Van,
still laughing gently. "Your friend's husband is a gambler, and no mistake. His

visits to the principal cities of Mexico are strictly professional. He has come to Aguas Calientes for the fair, and just at present he is the dealer at the table here in the hotel; that's the 'bank' he goes to every evening and stays at until three o'clock the next morning. And I don't doubt that every word his wife said about his domestic virtues was the literal truth. In his way Mr. Heintz-bach is a person of the utmost respectability; but—but perhaps when you see your friend again you might say something about our re-turn to New York being a little uncertain; and I don't think I'd say anything more about their visiting us, if I were you. If Mr. Heintzbach were on Wall Street, now, it would be all right; but as his game isn't in stocks, it might be as well—yes, I'm sure quite as well—for us to fight a little shy of him. But oh, Rose, my angel, what a delightful thing this is that you have done! And what a perfect howl there will be to-morrow when I tell how you and the gambler's wife have become sworn friends!"

"Van!" cried Rose, springing away from him and facing him with every sign of energy and determination, "if you ever breathe so much as the first syllable of this to anybody I'll—I'll drown myself!"

"No, don't drown yourself, Rose. Think how draggled you'd look. Do it, if you really think you must do it, in some way that will be becoming. Why, my poor little girl!"—Rose was beginning to sob—"it's wicked to laugh at you," and Brown succeeded by an heroic effort in mastering another outburst. "After all, it was a natural enough sort of thing to do; and nothing will come of it to bother you, child, for we shall leave here day after to-morrow, and of course you'll never lay eyes on the gambler's wife again; and I'll never speak about it to a soul, I give you my word. But—but don't you think there is something just a *little* funny in it all, Rose?"

It was one of the small trials of Vandyke Brown's life that his wife never saw the amusing side of this adventure. As for Mrs.

Heintzbach, she set down to the general queerness of Americans the peculiarity of Mrs. Brown's manner when, next day, she presented to that lady the promised letters to her Guanajuato relatives. For while Rose strove hard to maintain a tone of friendly cordiality, the underlying consciousness that she did not really want to be cordial and friendly rather marred the general result. Nor was Mrs. Heintzbach ever able to formulate a satisfactory hypothesis that would account for the fact that, while the American party certainly visited Guanajuato, the letters of introduction as certainly remained unused.

IV.

THE SKIRMISH AT BUENA VISTA.

MR. MANGAN BROWN and Mr. Gamboge investigated the tanneries of Leon with much interest. In regard to the quality of the raw-hides, they expressed entire approval; but their strictures upon the tanning process, and upon the product in dressed leather, were severe.

"I am glad that the late Mr. Orpiment is not with us, Brown," Mr. Gamboge remarked, with some feeling. "The mere sight of such sole-leather as we have been looking at this morning would have given him an attack of bilious dyspepsia; it would, upon my word! I regard tanning like this," he added, slowly and impressively, "as positively immoral. I am not at all surprised, Brown—not the least bit in the world surprised—that a nation that accords its tacit approval to tanning of this sort is incapable of achieving a stable government. I may add that I am sure that Mexico will lag behind all other nations in the march of progress until its leather business has been radically remodelled and reformed." And in this possibly extreme opinion Mr. Mangan Brown, who also was deeply moved by what he had seen, entirely concurred.

But the rest of the party, being blissfully ignorant of the tanning iniquities of Leon, were disposed to think the bustling little city altogether charming. Rowney Mauve described it happily as a mixture of the Bowery and the Middle Ages; young Orpiment delightedly made the studies for his well-known picture, "A Mexican Calzada"—the picture that made such a sensation when it subsequently was exhibited in New York; and while Brown was disappointed by his failure to discover so much as a single good picture in any of the churches, his heart was gladdened by finding all around him a rich abundance of material out of which good pictures might be made.

On the whole, the verdict of the party already was strongly in favor of Mexico; and after its several members had enjoyed the perfect picturesqueness of Guanajuato—where the noble paintings by Vallejo in the parish church, and the still finer work by Cabrera in the Compañia, suddenly opened the eyes of the artists to the greatness of Mexican art—this pleasing sentiment expanded into and thereafter remained (with the exceptions noted below) one of unmixed approval.

Mr. Pemberton Logan Smith avowedly pined for the flesh-pots of Philadelphia. "I am not at all particular about my food, you know, Mauve," he said, plaintively; "but hang it, you know, I do like a solid meal now and then; and except at that queer little place at Lagos, where things certainly were capital, I'll be shot if I've had a solid, well-cooked meal since I came into Mexico."

"Haven't you, though?" Mauve asked,

with a slight air of scepticism. "Now, I was under the impression that I had seen you several times doing some tolerably serious pecking. Anyhow, you stowed away enough at Lagos to last you till you get home again."

"Yes," Pem answered, "I did have some satisfactory feeding there. Jove! what a heaven-born genius in the cooking line that jolly old Gascon is! And don't I just wish that I knew where I could get as good a claret for as little money in Philadelphia or New York!" And Pem smacked his lips feelingly as he remembered Don Pedro's inspiring food and drink. But even sustained by this cheering memory, it was not until he was come to the City of Mexico and reposed, as it were, in the culinary bosom of Father Gatillon, at the Café Anglais, that Pem really was comforted.

The other exception in the matter of entire approval of Mexico was Mrs. Gamboge; and the point of issue in her case was a delicate one. To state it plainly, it was the bare legs of the agricultural laborers. In confidence she confessed to Verona that had she been informed of the custom of excessively rolling up their cotton trousers prevalent among the lower classes of male Mexicans she certainly would have remained at home.   What with this and the equally objectionable custom prevalent among the female Mexicans of the lower classes of insufficiently covering the upper portions of their bodies, Mrs. Gamboge declared that the average of dress among the lower classes of Mexico was reduced to a point considerably below that at which inadequacy of apparel became personally shocking and morally reprehensible.   And all the way from Silao to the City of Mexico — which journey, from point to point, was made by the day train—Mrs. Gamboge sat retired within her prison-like " drawing-room," her face resolutely turned away from the windows, and both the blinds close-drawn.   Not even the beautiful cañon south of Querétaro, not even the extraordinary loveliness of the Tula Valley, could tempt her forth from the rigid propriety of her retreat.

" Either the railroad company should take the necessary legal measures to compel these men to wear trousers as they are intended to be worn," Mrs. Gamboge declared, "or else it should build a high board fence on each side of the track." And neither from this decided opinion nor from her self-imposed seclusion could she be stirred.

It was with a feeling of some slight relief, therefore, that Mrs. Gamboge found herself, at the end of the long run from Querétaro, delivered from the prominent presence as a feature of the landscape of unduly bare-legged laborers by the arrival of the train at the Buena Vista station, in the City of Mexico. She thought it highly probable that other shocks might here await her; but she had at least the sustaining conviction that the male members of the Mexican lower classes dwelling in cities as a rule kept their trousers rolled down.

As the party moved away from their car toward the gates, at the farther end of the station, they passed the night express train

that in a few minutes would start for the
north.   A little group stood by the steps of
the Pullman car, and the central feature of
this group was a young woman whose travel-
ling-dress betokened the fact that she was
about to depart on the train.   "See what
stunning eyes she's got, Rose," Vandyke
Brown said, in a discreetly low tone, "and
look how well she carries herself.   I'd like to
paint her.   She'd make no end of an exhibition portrait."

Just at this moment Violet, who was a few
steps ahead of them, gave a little shriek; and
then the strange young woman gave a little
shriek; and then they rushed into each other's
arms.   Rowney, from whom Violet had broken away to engage in this rather pronounced
exhibition of affection, stood by placidly until
it should come to an end.   He was accustomed to Violet's rather energetic methods,
and in the present instance his only regret
was that he was not in the running himself.
But even Rowney's placidity was a little disturbed when Violet, having detached herself

from the young woman, proceeded, with a similar vehemence, to cast herself first into the arms of an elderly lady, then into those of an elderly gentleman, then into those of a middle-aged gentleman, and finally into the arms of two quite young gentlemen, all of whom embraced her with what Rowney considered, especially upon the part of the young men, most unnecessary fervor, the while patting her vigorously upon the back.

If Rowney had contemplated lodging a remonstrance in regard to this, from a New York standpoint, abnormal exhibition of friendship, he had no opportunity to do so. Before he could open his mouth Violet seized upon him and dragged him into the midst of the little group, where his demoralization for the time being was made complete by finding himself passed rapidly from one pair of arms to another, and embraced by these friendly strangers with quite as much enthusiasm as they had manifested in embracing his wife. During this confusing experience he was conscious that for a moment he was clasped in the soft arms of the handsome young woman, and realized, as he remembered his wish of but a moment before, that the fulfilment of human desires is not necessarily attended with perfect happiness.

"O Rowney!" cried Violet, "do be glad to see them; don't look so scandalized and horrified. They are ever so glad to see you. Don't you understand? This is my very dearest, dearest friend, Cármen Espinosa, and this is her uncle, Señor Antonio Ochoa, and this is his younger brother, Señor Manuel Ochoa, and this is her aunt, Doña Catalina—Don Antonio's wife, you know—and these are her cousins, Rafael and Rodolfo. Oh! isn't it perfectly delightful! And to think if our train hadn't come in exactly on time we should have missed them; for Cármen and all of them are going to Guanajuato to-night! And Violet once more threw herself into her friend Cármen's arms.

Meanwhile the American party had halted and had gazed at Violet's demonstrative proceedings with a very lively astonishment, that became a less serious emotion as they contemplated the ill grace with which Rowney suffered himself to be inducted into the amicable customs of Mexico.

"Upon my soul, Gamboge," said Mr. Brown in some alarm, "we'd better get out of this or Violet will be turning her friends loose at hugging us too. I hope that I should get through with the performance, with the pretty girl, anyway, better than young Mauve did, but there's no telling; and, I must say, I don't want to try." That Violet would have introduced her friends is quite certain, but just as she was about to begin this ceremony, and while Rowney was endeavoring to atone for his want of animation during the period of the embraces by making such civil speeches as were possible with the limited stock of Spanish at his command, the starting-bell sounded, and the Pullman conductor summoned the party with a firm civility to enter the train. This time, greatly to his relief, Rowney found that nothing more than an ordinary shaking of hands was expected of him; and as he knew in a general way the proper speeches to make on such an occasion, he got through with the business of leave-taking in fairly creditable form.

"Only you oughtn't to have said '*adios*,' Rowney," said Violet, correctingly. "That is the same thing as the French *adieu*, you know. You should have said '*hasta luego*,' for that means *au revoir;* and they had just told you that they would be back in the city in a week. It is dreadfully stupid the way in English you say just as much of a 'good-by' to a person you are going to see again in two hours as you say to a person who is just starting on a journey around the world. But isn't it lovely that we met them? And don't you think, Rowney, that Cármen is the dearest dear that ever was? It's the Cármen I've told you of a thousand times, Rowney; the one who was in the Sisters' school with me. If I were good at letter-writing I should have written to her every week; but I'm not very good that way, you know, and I don't believe she is either, and so we've never heard a single word about each other in two years. She didn't even know I was married; and when I said I was married to ' that handsome man there '—yes, I did say that, and you ought to be very much obliged to me, Rowney—and pointed to where you all were standing, she actually thought I meant Mr. Smith! Wasn't that a funny mistake? Mr. Smith certainly is a nice-looking man; but he is not so nice-looking as you are, Rowney, even if I do say it myself and puff you all up with conceit. And now do let us hurry to the hotel. I know that we'll get something good, and I'm so hungry that I could eat trunk-straps and top-boots, like the people who are wrecked and spend forty-seven days in an open boat at sea."

And as Violet's condition of incipient starvation was that of the whole party—for they had breakfasted at one o'clock in the afternoon at San Juan del Rio, and it was now after eight o'clock in the evening—the move toward the Café Anglais and dinner was made with the least possible delay.

Pem sat next to Violet at dinner, and before she had swallowed her soup he began to ask rather pointed questions about her charming Mexican friend.

"Now, I tell you frankly, Mr. Smith," Violet declared with much positiveness, "that until I have had something to eat I shall not say a single word. I have a perfectly clear conscience, and that means, of course, that I've got a good appetite; and I have. If you've got a bad conscience, and consequently a bad appetite, that's no fault of mine; and I don't intend to suffer for your sins. So, there!"

But even when Violet, having satisfied the cravings of hunger, was disposed to be communicative concerning her friend, her communication was eulogistic rather than informing. Beyond the fact that Cármen Espinosa belonged to very nice people whose home was an *hacienda* up in the Bajío, she had very little to tell. They had been together in the school of the Sagrado Corazon for two years. Then Violet had gone back to her father's *hacienda* in Michoacan; and a year later had gone on her expedition to New York, that had ended in keeping her there as the wife of Rowney Mauve. A letter or two during the first six months after their separation had been their only attempt at correspondence. Of her friend's life during the past two and a half years she knew nothing. But she was the best and sweetest and dearest girl that ever lived—and so on, and so on.

Pem was silent as he sat smoking with the other men over their coffee, after the ladies had retired up the corkscrew staircase to their rooms. There was some talk among the artists about the work that they intended doing; and presently Pem roused up and said:

"Well, I'll tell you what I'm going to do. I'm going to Guanajuato to paint that view of the Bufa from up by the highest of the *presas*. It's the finest thing I've seen in Mexico, and I mean to get it. I'm going to-morrow."

There was a stir of astonishment at this outburst of vigor on the part of Mr. Smith, and his announcement was met, not unnaturally, with comment tending toward skeptical criticism.

"I did think that you was resolvéd, Mr. Smeeth, not to touch one brush while in thees land," said Jaune d'Antimoine, seriously.

"And so did I," added Brown. "What's got into you, old man, to break down your virtuous resolution to be lazier than usual?"

"Look here, my dear fellow," Rowney Mauve put in, "I'd like to know what's to become of me if you take to working? Don't you see that I rely on you for moral support? But you don't mean it, I'm sure."

"I do mean it, and I tell you I'm going to-morrow. I've always meant to take home one picture from Mexico; at least I've always rather thought I would. And the more I think about that view of the Bufa, the more I'm determined that that shall be what I'll paint."

Pem had been known to make resolutions of this sort before without any very startling practical results ensuing, and not much faith was placed by anybody in his stout assertion. But faith was compelled, early the next evening, when he stated that he was about to have an early dinner in order to catch the north-bound train, and then bade everybody good-by. And off he went, with the parting shot from Brown that Saul among the prophets wasn't a touch to him.

In the privacy of their respective chambers that night Brown and Mauve expressed to their respective wives their astonishment at this extraordinary manifestation of energy on the part of their Philadelphia friend.

Rose smiled in a superior way and said: "Really, Van, I sometimes think that you are about as stupid as even a man can be! Why, don't you see that Mr. Smith has gone after that pretty Mexican girl?"

And Violet, in response to very similar utterances on the part of Rowney Mauve, very similarly replied: "What a thick-headed creature you are, Rowney. Mr. Smith has gone after Cármen, of course. I knew what he was up to at once, and I thought I'd help him a little, and so I—I asked him if it would be too much trouble, since he was going to Guanajuato anyway, to take a letter from me to my friend. And you just ought to have seen how very grateful the poor fellow was ! But you mustn't tell, Rowney; that wouldn't be the square thing."

THE AFFAIR OF MOLINO DEL REY.

MR. PEMBERTON LOGAN SMITH returned from Guanajuato five or six days later, bringing his sheaves with him. But his sheaves did not amount to much.

He arrived from the railway station in time to join the party at dinner; and although dining was about at an end, they all waited while he ate his dinner and at the same time gave an account of himself.

"What a blessing it is again to get something to eat," he observed with much satisfaction as Gilberto—"the best waiter I ever came across anywhere," Mr. Gamboge had declared approvingly—took away his empty soup-plate and filled his glass from a bottle of Father Gatillon's sound Bordeaux. "I stayed at Doña Maria's, of course, and the old lady did her best for me, I know—but even her best didn't amount to much; and I've been getting hungrier and hungrier every day."

"And how about the picture?" Brown asked. "You must have made pretty quick work of it to get anything done in this time."

"Oh, the picture! Yes, I'd forgotten about that. You see, when I saw the Bufa again I concluded that it was too much for me. It wants a bigger man, you know—somebody like Orpiment. You really ought to go up and paint it, Orpiment; it's a wonderful thing." This pleased Verona, of course. She highly approved of anything in the shape of an acknowledgment of her husband's superiority.

"That's all very well," said Orpiment; "but if you haven't been painting the Bufa, what have you been doing? And what's gone with all your virtuous resolutions?"

"Well, you see, we didn't half do up Guanajuato—it's a wonderful place; I think it's the most picturesque place I ever saw.

I've been investigating it. I found some more pictures, for one thing. There's a tremendously good 'Cena de San Francisco,' that we never saw at all, in the sacristy of that little church just across the street from Doña Maria's. And I went out to the Valenciana mine, and there is one of the most beautiful churrigueresque church interiors out there that I ever laid eyes on: and we missed that, too, you know. There was lots to do without painting. I could have put in another week easily."

"Did you see anything of the Espinosas?" Violet asked, with a fine air of innocent curiosity.

"The Espinosas? Oh, yes, I saw them. In fact I—as it happened, I saw a good deal of them," Pem answered, in some slight confusion. "Yes, they were very civil to me," he continued. "You see I had to present the letter that you sent, Mrs. Mauve; and when they found that I had missed so much that is worth seeing in Guanajuato they took me in hand in the kindest way and showed me everything. It was ever so nice of them. And—and we happened to come down together on the same train. You see, I found it was quite hopeless to try to paint the Bufa, and as they were coming down I thought I'd come down too. What a nice old lady the Señora Espinosa is, and Don Antonio is delightful. I've rarely met such pleasant people."

"And how about the pretty girl?" Brown struck in, although Rose tried to stop him by pinching him.

"It's never any good to pinch me, Rose," Brown explained, when his conduct subsequently was criticised. "Half the time I don't know what I'm pinched for, and it only makes me get my back up; and the other half you don't get in your pinch until I've said what you don't want me to say. If I were you I'd stop it."

"But, Van, indeed it was very unkind in you to speak that way to-night. Don't you see that Mr. Smith is quite seriously interested in this sweet young girl; and just suppose you were to make him so uncomfortable that he should break it all off before it's fairly· begun.   Don't do anything like that again, I beg of you."

"For so young a woman, Rose, your match-making proclivities are quite remarkable. How do you know that this Mexican girl is 'sweet'? Remember your gambling friend at Aguas Calientes, and don't be precipitate, my dear" (this was an unfair allusion on Brown's part, and he had to apologize for it). "After all, though, you must admit that Smith didn't seem to be very badly knocked out by my shot at him."

This was quite true, for Pem had expected some such question, and, being ready for it, he answered with a very fair degree of composure: "You mean the Señora Carillo. She is charming, of course. I don't believe that you know, Mrs. Mauve," he added, turning to Violet, "that your friend is a widow?"

"Oh, how perfectly delightful!" cried Violet. Then, seeing that Rose, Verona, and Mrs. Gamboge all looked shocked, she added:

"Of course I don't mean that it is delightful to have peoples' husbands die, or anything like that, you know. But after they *are* dead, in this part of the world at least, it's delightful to be a widow. A Mexican young girl might just as well be a—a humming-top, for all the good she has of anything, you see. But as soon as she's a widow she can go anywhere and do anything she pleases, and have nobody bothering at her at all. It's better than being a young girl in the States, ever so much. And so Cármen's a widow. Just think of it! And I didn't even know that she had been married. She's got ever so far ahead of me, hasn't she, Rowney? And I thought that I was ahead of her. It's too bad! But who did she marry, Mr. Smith? And when did he die? Do tell me all about it, please."

And Pem explained that the Señorita Espinosa had been married about a year after the time that she had left school, and that her husband had died suddenly within two or three months of their marriage. "I don't believe it was quite a heart-breaking affair," Pem added. "Her cousin, Rodolfo, you know, told me that old Don Ignacio was a grouty old fellow, and that the marriage had been made up mainly because his *hacienda* adjoined her father's, and there was some row about the water-rights which had been going on for years and which they succeeded this way in compromising. Rodolfo was very indignant about the whole business, and I'm sure I don't wonder. Do they do much of that sort of thing down here, Mrs. Mauve? It's like a bit out of the dark ages."

"But think how happy she is now, Mr. Smith," said the practical Violet; "and think what a good thing it is to have the matter about the water settled so nicely. You don't know how important it is to get a thing like that settled. I remember papa and another man had a bad shooting match about a water-right once; and papa would have been killed, everybody said, if he hadn't been too quick for the other man and got the drop on him. And it cost papa ever so much to square things after he'd killed the other man; for the judges knew that papa was rich and they made him pay like anything. I'm very glad for Cármen's sake that she was able to do her father such a good turn; and she must be glad too—especially now that it's all well over and she is a comfortable widow. And you say that they all came down with you to-night?"

"Yes, and they sent word that they are coming in a body to call on all of us to-morrow—that's the Mexican way, I believe. And they have a plan on foot for a picnic, or something of that sort, for us at Señor Espinosa's place out at Tacubaya——"

"Oh, in that lovely garden! I used to go out there with Cármen sometimes on Sundays while I was at the convent. It's perfectly delightful!"

"Yes, I fancy from what they said about it that it must be rather a nice place. And after the lunch, or breakfast, or whatever they call it, we're to walk across and see the view of the valley from a place that they say is very nice—it's upon a hillside above the Molino del Rey; just where the battle was fought in 1847, Don Antonio said. Really, Mrs. Mauve, we all owe a great deal to you for putting us in the way of seeing Mexican life from the inside."

This view of the indebtedness of the American party to the Spanish-American member became general two days later, when they all were conveyed to Tacubaya by Don Antonio in a special tram-car, and were given a breakfast in his beautiful *huerta* that quite astonished them. That Pem approved of the food, Philadelphian though he was, did not, under the circumstances, count for much; but the hearty indorsement of Mexican cooking on the part of Mr. Gamboge and Mr. Mangan Brown, neither of whom regarded such matters lightly, and whose judgment was not biassed by any sudden yielding to the tender emotions, counted for a good deal. It was while they were returning to the city that Mr. Gamboge, after a long, thoughtful silence, thus spoke:

"Brown, I shall remember that dish of *mole*—I have learned the name of it carefully, you see—until my dying day."

And Mr. Mangan Brown briefly but feelingly replied: "And so shall I."

As for Rose, she declared that she must be asleep and had dreamed herself into a Watteau landscape; for such a garden as this was, as she lucidly explained, she believed could have no existence outside of a picture that was inside of a dream.

Mrs. Gamboge, whose tendency was toward the sentimental, wished Mr. Gamboge to come and sit beside her on the grass, beneath a tree near the little brook. And her feelings were rather hurt because Mr. Gamboge declined to fall in with her romantic fancy, on the ground that sitting on the grass certainly would give them both rheumatism. And he didn't mend matters by adding that he would have been very glad to please her had they only thought to bring along a gum-blanket.

But quite the happiest member of this

exceptionally happy party was Mr. Pemberton Logan Smith; for this young man, while
he was not as yet exactly in love, had made
a very fair start into the illusions and en-
tanglements of that tender passion.   During
the four or five days at Guanajuato his inter-
course with the Señora Carillo had been
hampered by the formalities attending new
acquaintanceship, and especially by the rule
of Mexican etiquette that throws the entertainment of a guest upon the oldest lady of
the household.   His eyes had been very
steadily in the service of the pretty widow;
but his ears, and so much of his tongue as
the circumstances of the case required—which
was not much, for Doña Catalina was a great
talker—necessarily were employed in the
service of her aunt.

But on the present occasion Doña Catalina
naturally devoted herself more especially to
Mrs. Gamboge and the two elderly gentlemen—Violet, rather against her will, serving
as interpreter—and this left Pem free to follow his own inclinations.   It was the first fair

chance that he had had, and he made the most of it. A further fortunate fact in his favor was that he was the only man of the American party—except Jaune d'Antimoine, who was busily employed as interpreter between his wife, Rose, Verona, and the Mexican young gentlemen—who possessed a colloquial command of Spanish. How Pem did bless his lucky stars now that, being overtaken by a mood of unwonted energy, he had had the resolution to grind away so steadily under that stuffy old professor during his winter in Granada!

So, without much difficulty, he contrived to keep close to the widow all day—much to his own enjoyment, and, apparently, not to her distaste. She was not like any of the women whom he had known in Spain— where, to be sure, his opportunities for any save most formal acquaintance had been very limited; and she certainly was unlike her own countryfolk. Even in her lightest talk there was an air about her of preoccupation, of reserve, that was in too marked contrast with Doña Catalina's very cheerful frankness to be accounted for merely on the ground of the difference between youth and age; and that, so far as his observation had gone, was not by any means characteristic of Mexican women either old or young. And from the obscurity of this reserve she had a way, he found, of flashing out rather brilliantly turned expressions of decidedly original thought. When she accompanied these utterances, as she sometimes did, with a little curl of her finely cut red lips, and with a quick glance from her dark-brown eyes—not tender eyes, yet eyes which somehow suggested possibilities of tenderness—he found that her sayings, if not increased in point, certainly gained in effectiveness. Altogether, Mr. Smith was disposed to regard the Señora Carillo as a decidedly interesting subject for attentive study.

Naturally, since they had been so much together during the day, Pem was the widow's escort when they all set out, in late afternoon, to walk to the point of view that Don

Antonio, as he expressed it, would have the honor to bring to their notice. It was a desperately dusty walk, and the American ladies—who had donned raiment of price for the occasion—contemplated the defilement of their gowns in anything but a contented spirit. They beheld with wonder the calmness with which their Mexican sisters—who were equally well dressed, though in the style that would obtain in New York during the ensuing season—made no effort whatever to preserve their garments from contamination.

"That gros-grain of Mrs. Espinosa's will be absolutely ruined, Rose," Mrs. Gamboge declared, speaking in the suppressed voice that most people seem to consider necessary when airing their private sentiments in the presence of other people who do not understand a word of the language in which the private sentiments are expressed. "Mine is bad enough, though I'm doing everything I can think of to save it. Do just drop behind me a little and see if I'm making a very shocking exhibition of my ankles. I'm afraid that

I am, but I really can't help it. These Mexican ladies seem to think no more of getting dusty than if they all were dressed in calico. I can't understand it at all."

The Señora Carillo certainly paid no attention whatever to the increasing dustiness of her gown. Her early venture in matrimony had not been of an encouraging sort, and since she had come into her estate of widowhood her tendency—as Violet in her free but expressive southwestern vernacular probably would have stated the case—was to "stand off" mankind generally. It was a surprise to herself when she discovered that so far from finding this good-looking young *Americano* repulsive, she positively was attracted by him. For one thing, he struck her as differing in many ways from her own countrymen; and she had an instinctive feeling that the unlikeness was not merely superficial. She was sure that his scheme of life was a larger, broader scheme than that which she had known, and there was a genuineness in his deference to her as a woman that contrasted both forcibly and favorably with certain of her past experiences.

In point of fact this Mexican young woman had begun life by being a little out of harmony with her environment. She did not know very clearly what she wanted, but she knew that it was something quite different from that which she had. It was this feeling that had led her to select Violet Carmine for a close friend. She was not at all in sympathy with Violet's most radical tendencies; but she found in Violet a person, the only person, who was not shocked when she stated some of her own small convictions as to what a woman's life might be. Even to this friend she had not told that it was her hope, should she ever marry, to be the companion of her husband—not merely his handmaiden, in the scriptural sense. And she was glad now that she had been thus reticent, for her hope by no means had been realized.

After that very disillusioning venture into the holy estate of matrimony, this poor Cár-men found herself entirely at odds with herself and with the world. Had she lived a generation earlier she would have become a nun. It was a subject of sincere sorrow to her that nunneries had been abolished in Mexico by the Laws of the Reform.

It was only natural that there should be a certain feeling of pleasure mixed with her feeling of astonishment at her present discovery of a man for whom she had at once both liking and respect. It was agreeable, she thought, to find that there really was such a man in the world. But beyond this very general view of the situation her thoughts did not go. It made very little difference to her, one way or the other, this discovery. The man was a foreigner, and an American at that —and Cármen had a good strong race hatred for the Americans of the North—come into her country only for a little while. Presently he would go home again ; and that, so far as she was concerned, would be the end of him. In the meantime she would please herself by studying this new specimen of male humanity. It was well to hold con-

verse with a foreigner, she thought; it en-
larged one's mind.

So, lagging a little behind the rest of the
party, and chatting in a manner somewhat
light to be productive of any very marked
mental improvement, they walked westward
through the straggling streets of Tacubaya
—past low houses with great barred windows,
past high-walled gardens, the loveliness of
which was only hinted at by outhanging
trees and climbing vines and by the glimpse
in passing to be had through the iron gates
—over to and out upon the hillside above
the Molino del Rey. They stopped beside
the little pyramidal monument that com-
memorates the battle. The rest of the party had gone on a few rods farther; for Don
Antonio, with true Mexican courtesy, had
acted upon his instinctive conviction that beside this monument was not a place where
a party of right-thinking Americans would
care to halt.

Below them, embowered in trees, was the
old Mill of the King that Worth's forces car-

ried that September day forty years ago; beyond rose the wooded, castle-crowned height of Chapultepec; still farther away were the towers and glistening domes of the city and the great shimmering lakes, and for background rose the blue-gray mountains above Guadalupe in the north. To the east, over across Lake Chalco, towered the great snow-peaks of the volcanoes.

" Upon my soul, I wish I had been born a Mexican," said Pem, drawing a long breath.

" Because the Mexicans happen to be possessors of a fine landscape? That is not a good reason. There are better things for a people to have than landscapes, Señor; and some of these better things, if I am rightly told, your people have."

" It is possible—but at present I cannot recall them to my mind. Just now I can think of nothing finer than this view—excepting the happy fact that the Señorita has done me the honor to lead me to it."

" I could wish that you would not speak in that fanciful manner. It is in the custom of my own country, and I do not like it. I have been told that the Americans do not make fine speeches, and I shall be glad to know that it is so."

Pem was rather taken aback by this frank statement of very un-Mexican sentiment.

" The Señorita, then, does not approve of the customs of her own people, and is pleased to like the Americans ? For the compliment to my countrymen I give to the Señorita my thanks."

" I do not like your countrymen. I hate them."

" And why ?"

" Is not this an answer ?" Cármen replied, laying her hand upon the battle monument.

Pem felt himself to be in an awkward corner, for the position that his Mexican friend had taken—while not, perhaps, in the very best of taste—was quite unassailable. As he rather stupidly stared at the ugly little monument, thus pointedly brought to his notice, he felt that it did indeed represent an act of unjust aggression that very well might make

Mexicans hate Americans for a thousand years.

" As to the customs of my countrymen," Cármen continued, perceiving that the particular American before her was very much embarrassed, and politely wishing to extricate him from the trying position that, not very politely, she had placed him in, " some of them are very well. But this of making fine speeches to women is not well at all. Do the men have this foolish custom in your land, or is it only that while in Mexico you wish to do what is done here ? "

It was a relief to have the subject changed in any way, but the new topic was one not altogether free from difficulties. Mr. Smith never before had been called upon to defend the utterance of a small gallantry upon ethical and ethnological grounds; still less to treat the matter from the standpoint of comparative nationalities.

" It is my impression that I have heard of handsome speeches being made upon occasion by American men to American women," he replied. "Yes, I believe that I am justified in saying positively that speeches of this sort among us may be said to be quite every-day affairs. May I ask why the Señorita objects to them? They strike me as being harmless, to say the least."

"They are idle and silly. It is the same talk that one would give to a cat. I do not know why a woman should be talked to as though she had nothing of sense. It is true, she cannot know as much as a man ; but she may ask to have it believed that she knows more than a cat, and still not claim to be very wise. And so, if the Señor will permit the request, I will beg that he will keep his handsome speeches for those who like them and that he will say none to me at all.

"See, our friends are coming toward us, and we will go back to the town. And the Señor will pardon me if I have been rude. I should not have said what I did about Americans. I find now that they are not all bad." There was more in the look that accompanied this utterance than there was in the words.

"I have not had a very happy life, and sometimes, they tell me, I forget to be considerate of others and am unkind. But I have not meant to be unkind to-day."

The last portion of Cármen's speech was hurried, for the party was close upon them, and they all were together again before Pem could reply.

Nor did he have another chance to continue this, as he had found it, notwithstanding the awkward turns that it had taken, very interesting conversation. Cármen stuck close to her aunt, and was almost silent, as they walked back to the garden; and she contrived, as they returned by the tramway to the city, to seat herself quite away from him in the car.

Since she so obviously had no desire to speak further, Pem felt that he would be pleasing her best by engaging the estimable Doña Catalina in lively talk. This was not a difficult feat, for Doña Catalina was a miracle of good-natured loquacity, who, in default of anything better to wag her tongue at, no doubt would have talked with much animation to her shoes. In view of the fact that he scarcely had been able to get in a word edgewise, he was rather tickled when this admirable woman, at parting, commended him warmly for having so well mastered the Spanish tongue. Pem ventured, at this juncture, to cast a very slightly quizzical look at Cármen, and was both surprised and delighted by finding that his look was returned in kind.

"A Mexican woman who doesn't like pretty speeches, and who has such a charming way of qualifying her hatred of Americans, and who can see the point of a rather delicate joke," thought Pem, "would be worth investigating though she were sixty years old and as ugly as the National Palace. And Cármen"—this was the first time, by the way, that he had thought of her as Cármen—"I take it is not quite twenty yet; and what perfectly lovely eyes she has!"

At dinner that night Mr. Smith was unusually silent. When rallied by the lively Violet upon his taciturnity he replied that he was rather tired.

VI.

THE BATTLE OF CHURUBUSCO.

WHEN the American party played the return match, as Rowney Mauve, who had cricketing proclivities, expressed it, by giving their Mexican friends a breakfast in the pretty San Cosme Tivoli, Cármen did not appear. She had a headache that day, her aunt explained, and begged to be excused.

Rose commented upon this phase of the breakfast with her usual perspicacity. "I think that it all is working along very nicely, Van, don't you?" They had strolled off together and were out of ear-shot of the rest of the party.

"What is working along nicely? The breakfast? Yes, it seems to be all right. The food was very fair, and our friends seemed to enjoy themselves after their customary rather demonstrative fashion."

"It is a great trial to me, Van, the way you never catch my meaning. I don't mean the breakfast at all ; I mean about Mr. Smith and this lovely widow. Isn't it queer to think that she is a widow ? Except that she has a serious way about her—that has come to her through her sorrow, of course, poor dear !— nobody ever would dream that she was anything but a young girl. What a romance her life has been ! "

" Well, I can't say that I see much romance about it. First she was traded off by her father for a hydrant, or something of that sort ; and then she had an old husband—a most objectionable old beast he must have been from what we have heard about him—die on her hands before she was much more than married to him. I should say that the whole business was much less like a romance than like a nightmare. And as to this new match that you have made up for her working along nicely, it strikes me that just now it is work-

ing along about as badly as it can work.
Didn't you see how Smith went off into the
dumps the moment that he found his widow
had stayed at home? And don't you think
that her staying at home this way is the best
possible proof that she doesn't care a button
for him? Smith saw it quick enough, and
that was what made him drop right down
into dumpiness. So would I, if I'd been him,
and a girl had gone back on me that way.
You used to come and take walks with me,
Rosekin—in the old days when we were
spooning in Greenwich—when your head was
aching fit to split, you precious child." They
were in an out-of-the-way part of the garden,
and on the strength of this memory Brown
put his arm around his wife and kissed her.
After which interlude he added : " So can't
you see that all your match-making is moon-
shine? It's a case of ' he loved the lady, but
the lady loved not him,' and you might as
well accept the situation and stop your castle-
building."

" You are a very dear boy, Van, and of

course I'd go walking with you even without any head at all. But about love-matters you certainly are very short-sighted. You can't help it, I suppose, because you're a man ; and men never understand these things at all. But any woman could tell you at a glance that this love affair between Mr. Smith and the dear little Mexican widow is going on splendidly. Even you can see that Mr. Smith is in love with her. Well, I don't think that she's exactly in love with him yet ; but I am quite certain that she feels that if she doesn't take care she will be. That's the reason she had a headache and didn't come to-day."

"What a comfort it would be to Smith to know that!" Brown remarked with fine irony. "You had better tell him, my dear."

"Yes, of course it would be," Rose answered, entirely missing the irony. "And I've been thinking that I would tell him, Van ; only I thought that perhaps you wouldn't like me to. I'm very glad you won't mind— for of course he doesn't see, men are so stupid about such things. Suppose we go and hunt him up now, and then you go away and leave us together, and I'll tell him how much encouragement she is giving him."

"Suppose you tell me first. I'll be shot if I see much that's encouraging in her shying off from him this way."

"Why, I *have* told you, Van. It's because she is afraid that if she sees any more of him she really will fall in love with him; and of course, after her dreadful experience with that horrid old man she has made up her mind that she never will marry again. That is the way that any nice girl would feel about it. And of course, if she's so much interested in Mr. Smith that she won't trust herself to see him, it is perfectly clear that he has made a very good start toward getting her to love him. What we must do now is to help him——"

"Steady, Rose; don't go off your head, my child. This isn't our funeral."

"It *is* our funeral. Why, it's anybody's funeral who can help in a case of this sort. Think how much we owe to dear Verona for the way that she helped us. Certainly we must help him.   And the first thing for us to do is to give him another good chance to have a talk with her. That's all they want at present. No doubt we can do some other things later; and we will, of course. Why, Van, how can you be so heartless as not to be ready to do everything in your power to help your friend when the whole happiness of his life is at stake! And think what a good thing it will be for this poor sweet, broken-hearted girl, whose life has gone all wrong, to make it go right again."

Mrs. Brown's strongest characteristic was not, perhaps, moderation.   In the present instance, while her husband was not wholly convinced by her vigorous line of argument, he found her enthusiasm rather contagious.

"What are you going to do about it?" he asked, a little doubtfully.

"Why, I think we can manage just what has to be done now, getting them together again, you know, this way: You know Don Antonio has on hand an expedition for us to that beautiful old convent that he has been talking about, where there is such lovely tile-work, out at Churubusco. We had better arrange things now to go day after to-morrow. And to-morrow Mr. Smith shall send a note to Don Antonio telling him that he is very sorry to miss the expedition, but that he has decided to go up to see a friend in Toluca. He has been talking about that engineer up at Toluca whom he used to go to school with, so Don Antonio will think it all right and perfectly natural. And that will fix things beautifully. For then she'll go, of course."

"I don't see how it will fix anything beautifully for him to go off to Toluca. He won't see his widow there."

"O you foolish boy! He won't stay there, of course. He must go, because if he didn't he wouldn't be telling the truth in his note to Don Antonio"—Rose had a very nice regard for the truth—"but instead of staying at least one night, as of course they will expect him to, he must come right back to

Mexico by the afternoon train.   And then
he can tell Don Antonio, when we all meet
at the car as we did the other day, that he
has returned on purpose to join his party;
and that will please Don Antonio—and then
it will be too late for her to back out. And if
he needs any help to get her off to himself
when we are out at the convent, he can de-
pend upon me to see that he gets it!   Isn't
that a pretty good plan, Van ?   How delightful and exciting it all is!   It's almost as
though we were overcoming difficulties and
obstacles and getting married again ourselves,
isn't it, dear ?"

"No, I don't think it is. I think it's mainly
vigorous imagination let loose upon a very
small amount of fact.   But we'll play your little game, Rose, just for the fun of the thing.
Only there's one thing, child, that you must
be careful about.   You can't make your plan
go without explaining it to Smith.   Now
don't you tell him all the nonsense you have
been telling me about the way you think the
widow feels toward him. I don't think it's so;

and since he really seems to be rather hard hit, it isn't fair to set him up with a whole lot of hopes and then have things turn out the other way and knock him down again. Tell him that it is just barely possible that things are the way you think they are, and that your plan is in the nature of an experiment that probably will have no result at all, or will turn out altogether badly — as I certainly think it will. I don't believe that you can do him any good; but if you put the matter to him this way at least you won't do him any harm."

And Rose, perceiving the justice of her husband's utterance, promised him that in her treatment of this delicate affair she would be very circumspect indeed.

The first part of the plan thus skilfully elaborated worked to a charm. When the Americans joined Don Antonio and his party on the Plaza, to take the special tram-car in waiting for them on the Tlalpam tracks, Rose gave Van a delighted nudge and whispered:

"See, she has come, just as I said she would. And oh! oh!"— Rose squeezed Van's arm in her excitement with what he considered quite unnecessary vigor — "she has just seen Mr. Smith, and she is, indeed she is, changing color! Don't you see it? Now you know that I was right all along."

Brown, being on the lookout for it, did perceive this sign of confusion on the part of the Señora Carilla; but it was so slight that no one else, Pem alone excepted, noticed it. Another good sign, as Rose interpreted it, was that while Don Antonio and the rest were running over with voluble expressions of their pleasure because the Señor Esmit— the first letter and the digraph in Pem's name were too much for them—had cut short his visit to his friend in Toluca in order to join them in their outing, Cármen maintained a discreet silence. Pem, not being gifted with special powers of tortuous penetration, regarded this silence as ominous, until Rose, perceiving that he was going wrong, managed to whisper to him cheeringly : " It's all right. Quick, go and sit by her ! "

But this friendly advice came too late to be acted upon. Cármen, possibly foreseeing Pem's intention, executed a rapid flank movement—that Rose thought made the case still more hopeful, and that Pem thought made it still more hopeless—by which she placed herself securely between her aunt and her cousin Rodolfo, and so decisively checked the enemy's advance.

Under these discouraging circumstances Pem fell back on his reserve—that is to say, on Rose ; who made a place for him to sit beside her and, so far as this was possible without being too marked in her confidences, said what she could to cheer and comfort him.

And, indeed, this young gentleman's requirements in the way of cheering and comforting were very considerable. He had confided freely in Rose—who was a most refreshingly sympathetic confidante in a love affair—after she herself had broken the ice for him ; and the very fact of talking to her about his heart troubles had done a good deal to give them substance and directness. As the result of several conversations, Rose arrived at the conclusion that if Cármen had come to the breakfast at San Cosme, and had treated Pem in an every-day, matter-of-fact sort of way, the affair very likely would have been there and then ended. "But when I went to breakfast, and she was not there, Mrs. Brown," Pem exclaimed, "I suddenly realized how dreadfully much I had counted upon seeing her, and what a hold she had upon me generally. And then, while I was wretchedly low in my mind about it all, you came to me like an angel and told me that perhaps I had something to hope for. I shouldn't have hoped at all if it hadn't been for you. I think that I might even have had sense enough just to let it all go, and started right back for the States. And that would have been the end of it. But now that you have encouraged me, I'm quite another man. I shall fight it out now till she absolutely throws me over, or till I marry her.

"In the matter of family, Mrs. Brown," Pem went on, his Philadelphia instincts asserting themselves, "the marriage is a very desirable one. Her people have been established in América even longer than mine. Her cousin tells me that they trace their ancestry directly to the Conqueror himself— through the Cortés Tolosa line, you know— and they are connected with some of the very best families of Mexico and Spain. So, you see, there is no reason why I should not make her my wife. If it can be done, I'm going to do it; and if it can't—well, if it can't, there won't be much left in my life that's worth living for, that's all."

When Rose reported this conversation to her husband he listened with an air of serious concern. "You've shoved yourself into a tolerably good-sized responsibility, Rose," he said; "and I'm inclined to think, my child, that you're going to make a mess of it. I should advise you, if you are lucky enough to get out of this scrape with a whole skin, to take it as a sort of solemn warning that in future you will save yourself a good deal of trouble if you will let other people's love-making alone. But since you are so far in, my dear, I don't see how you can do any-thing but go ahead and try to bring Smith out all right on the other side."

Rose would not admit, of course, that she felt at all overpowered by the weight of her responsibility; but she did feel it, at least a little, and consequently hailed with a very lively satisfaction every act on Cármen's part that possibly could be construed as support-ing the hopeful view of the situation that she so energetically avowed. She went into the fight with all the more vigor now that victory was necessary not only to the happiness of her ally, but to the vindication of her own reputation as the projector of heart-winning campaigns.

Rose was encouraged by the fact that the tactics of the enemy were distinctly defen-sive. She argued that this betrayed a con-sciousness, possibly only instinctive, but none the less real, of forces insufficient to risk a general engagement; and she further argued that the most effective plan of attack would be to cut off the main body of the enemy (that is to say, Cármen herself) from her reserves (that is to say, from the protection of her aunt and other relatives) and then to force a decisive battle. Before the car reached San Mateo she had communicated this plan to Pem, and he had agreed to it.

But it is one thing to plan a campaign in the cabinet, and it is quite another thing to carry on the campaign in the field. The allies presently had this fact in military science pointedly brought home to them.

From where the car was stopped, near the little old parish church of San Mateo—closed now and falling into ruin, for the near-by conventual church has been used in its stead—the party walked a short half-mile along a lane bordered by magueys, and then came out upon a *plazuela* whereon the main gate of the convent opened. In the middle of the *plazuela* Pem saw, much to his disgust, another pyramidal battle monument, inscribed, like the one at Molino del Rey, with a brief eulogy of Mexican valor as shown in the gallant but futile resistance offered to the invading armies of the Americans of the North. It was very unlucky, he thought, that their expeditions should be directed so persistently to the old battle-fields of that wretched war. Since Cármen's pointed reference to the war, he had bought a Mexican school history and had read up on it; and even allowing for the natural bias of the historian, the more that he read about the part played by his own country the more was he ashamed of his own countrymen. Yet he could not but think also that it was rather hard that he should have to bear such a lot of responsibility for an event that occurred before he was born. It wasn't fair in Cármen, he thought, to liven up a dead issue like that and then to make it so confoundedly personal.

A couple of Mexican soldiers, in rather draggled linen uniforms, were sitting sentry lazily at the convent gate; and Don Antonio explained that the convent proper was now a military hospital. The church, and the large close in front of it, remained devoted to religious purposes, he said; and that portion of the old convent which inclosed the inner quadrangle had been reserved as a dwelling-place for the parish priest.

Passing to the left and turning the angle in the wall, they came to an arched gateway approached by a short flight of stone steps; and through this stately entrance, albeit somewhat shorn of its stateliness by the ruinous condition of its great wooden doors, they entered, and descended another short flight of steps into the close.

"Where are your Italian convents now?" Brown asked, turning to Rowney Mauve, who that morning had been talking rather airily about Italian convents. "You admitted as we came along how good this place was in mass—not scattered a bit, but all the lines well worked together—and how well the gray and brown of the walls, and the green of the trees, and the blue and white tiling of the dome, come together. Now we have some detail. Did you ever strike anything in Italy better than this great high-walled close, with its heavy shadows from these stunning trees and from the church and the convent, and its bits of color from these stations of the cross in colored tiles ? The church might be better, but it has at least a certain heavy grandeur, and the little tower up there is capital. And look how well those black arches close beside it bring out that perfectly beautiful little chapel—I suppose it is a chapel—completely covered with blue and yellow tiles! There are, no doubt, grander churches than this in Italy, and in several other places; but I'll be shot if I believe that there are any more perfectly picturesque or more entirely beautiful. Smith, just tell Don Antonio that I shall be grateful to him to the end of my days for having shown me this lovely place."

"He says that the cloister is finer," Pem translated, while Don Antonio's face beamed thanks upon the party at large; for all the

Americans manifestly concurred in Brown's enthusiastic expression of opinion. "And he says that the finest tile-work is in the choir. I must say I don't remember anything in Spain better than this. It's the rich, subdued color of it all, and the light and shade, I suppose, that does the business. I don't think it would paint, though; do you, Orpiment?"

"No, I don't. You could make a pretty good picture of it; but the picture wouldn't go for much with anybody who had seen the original. You can't paint a place that goes all around you, the way that this does; and you can't paint the spirit and the feeling of it—at least I can't; and that's what you'd have to get here if you got anything at all. No, this is one of the places that we'd better let alone."

The decision, which was a wise one, having been arrived at, the party passed under the archway beside the tiled chapel and so entered the inner quadrangle, surrounded by an arched cloister two stories high, the walls wainscoted with blue and white tiles. In the open, sunny centre was a little garden, and in the midst of the garden a curious old stone fountain in which purely transparent water bubbled up from a spring with such force as to make a jet three or four inches high above the centre of the large pool. The bubbling water glittered in the sunlight, and little waves that seemed half water and half sunshine constantly went out from the throbbing centre of the pool and fell away lightly upon its inclosing quaintly carved walls of stone.

Here there was another outburst of admiration on the part of the Americans, and while they were in the midst of it the parish priest, attracted by the sound of so many voices in this usually silent and forgotten place, came forth from a low archway and stared about him wonderingly. He was a little round man, with a kindly, gentle face, and a simplicity of manner that told of a pure soul and a trustful heart. Mrs. Gamboge, who entertained tolerably strong convictions in regard to the Scarlet Woman, and who heretofore had held as a cardinal matter of faith that every Roman Catholic priest was a duly authorized agent of the Evil One, found some difficulty in reconciling with these sound Protestant views the look and manner, and such of the talk as was translated to her, of this simple-minded, single-hearted man.

When it was made clear to the little Padre that this distinguished company, including even Americans from the infinitely remote city of New York, had come to look at his church because it was beautiful, his expression of mingled amazement and delight was a joy to behold. It had never occurred to him, he said, that anybody but himself should think of his poor church as beautiful. He had thought it so for a long while, ever since he had been brought to this parish from his former parish of Los Reyes : where the church was very small and very shabby, and, moreover, was tumbling down. But he had thought that his feeling for the beauty of his church was only because he loved it so well; for in all the years that he had been there no one ever had even hinted that it was anything more than churches usually are. Yet, it had seemed to him, he said modestly, that there was something about the way the shadows fell in the morning in the close, and something at that time about the colors of the walls and the richer color of the tiles, the like of which he had not seen elsewhere. In the stillness and quiet, amid these soft shadows and soft colors, somehow he found that his heart became so full that often, without at all meaning to pray, he would find his thoughts shaping themselves in prayer.

"Good for the Padre," said Orpiment, when Pem translated this to him. "That's the part of that picture that I said couldn't be painted. He doesn't look it a bit, but that little round man is an artist." But Orpiment was mistaken. Padre Romero loved beautiful things not because he was an artist, but because he had a simple mind and a pure soul.

Under the Padre's guidance the party entered the church—commonplace within, for reformation had destroyed its seventeenth-century quaintness—and thence passed up through the convent to the choir. This beautiful place, rich in elaborate tile-work, remained intact; and even the great choir-books, wrought on parchment in colored inks, still rested on the faldstool, waiting for the brothers to cluster around them once again in song. And there were the benches whereon the brothers once had rested; the central chair, in which their Father Saint Francis had sat in effigy; and to the right of this the chair of the Father Guardian. But the brothers had departed forever: legislated out of existence by the Laws of the Reform.

Rose gave a little shudder as she looked about her in this solemn, deserted place; and with her customary clearness of expression declared that it was "something like being in a deserted tomb full of Egyptian mummies."

"And to think," said Mr. Mangan Brown, who was a martyr to sea-sickness, "that Americans are constantly crossing that beastly Atlantic Ocean in search of the picturesque when things like this are to be seen dry-shod almost at their doors. Let us have our breakfast at once."

There was a lack of consecutiveness about Mr. Brown's remark, but its abstract comment and concrete suggestion were equally well received. Even Rowney Mauve, who was disposed to be critical, admitted that there were "several things worth looking at in Mexico," and added, by way of practical comment upon Mr. Brown's practical proposal, that he was as hungry as a bear.

All this while Rose had been endeavoring to bring about the *tête-à-tête* between Pem and Cármen that she believed would tend to the accomplishment of their mutual happiness. But her efforts had been unsuccessful. Cármen's defensive tactics no longer admitted of doubt, and even Rose was beginning to think that her sanguine interpretation of their meaning might be open to question. Thus far she had tried to cut Cármen out from her supports. She determined now to attempt the more difficult task of drawing off these supports, and so leaving Cármen isolated.

The breakfast, a very lively meal eaten in the lower cloister to the accompaniment of the tinkling of water falling from the fountain, gave her the desired opportunity for organizing her forces. With the intelligent assistance of Violet, who was taken into partial confidence because her knowledge of Spanish made her a valuable auxiliary, Rose contrived to break up the party, when breakfast was ended, so that she, Doña Catalina, Cármen, and Pem remained together, while the others scattered to explore the convent. Then, Pem serving as interpreter, she asked the ladies if it would be possible to walk in the tangled old garden that they had seen from a window in the sacristy.

Doña Catalina, being devoted to gardens, as Mexican women usually are, accepted the proposition immediately and heartily; and Cármen—a little uneasily, Rose thought— fell in with the plan. Fortunately the Padre appeared at this moment, and was delighted to guide them through a long dark corridor and so into his domain of trees and flowers. He was full of enthusiasm about the garden. It had been restored to the church only a month before, he said, after belonging to the hospital ever since the property had been confiscated. The soldiers had done nothing with it. The ladies could see for themselves its neglected state. They must come again in a year's time, and then they would see one of the finest gardens in the world. And full of delight, the little man explained with great volubility his plans for pruning and training, for clearing away weeds and rubbish, and for making his wilderness once more to blossom like the rose. Doña Catalina, having her own notions about gardens, entered with much animation into his plans, and they talked away at a great rate.

So Rose and Pem and Cármen walked through the shady alleys slowly, while Doña Catalina and the priest, walking still more slowly, and stopping here and there, that the projected improvements might be fully explained, dropped a long way behind.

It was a perfect Mexican day. Overhead was a clear, very dark-blue sky; liquid sunshine fell warmly through the cool, crisp air; a gentle wind idled along easily among the branches of the trees. The garden was very still. The only sound was a low buzzing of bees among the blossoms, and the faint gurgle of the flowing water in conduits unseen amidst the trees.

Rose stepped aside to pluck a spray of peach-blossoms. Cármen half stopped, but Pem, with admirable presence of mind, walked slowly on without pausing in the rather commonplace remark that he happened to be making in regard to the advantages of irrigation. A few steps farther on they came to a half-ruined arbor. They turned here and looked back along the alley, but Rose was not in sight. "She will join us in a moment," said Pem. "She is looking for flowers—she is very fond of flowers. Shall we wait for her here? And will the Señorita seat herself in the shade?"

Cármen stood for a moment irresolute. As

the result of what she believed to be a series of small accidents, she found herself now in precisely the situation that she had determined to avoid—alone with this *Americano* whom she had decided in her own mind to keep at a safe distance. Yet now that the situation that she had tried hard to render impossible actually had been brought about she found in it a certain excitement in which pleasure was blended curiously with pain. Her position certainly was weakened, for Pem observed, and counted the sign a good one, that her color had increased and that her eyes were brighter even than usual. She herself was conscious that the attack now had passed inside the skirmish line, and made an effort—not a very vigorous one—to rally her forces.

"Señorita! Señorita!" she called, but not very loudly, and her voice lacked firmness. There was no answer.

"She will be here in a moment," Pem repeated. "It is pleasant in this shady place. Will not the Señorita seat herself?   And will she answer me one question ?" Pem's own heart was getting up into his throat in an awkward sort of way, and his voice was not nearly so steady as he wished it to be. But the chance had come that he had been waiting for, and he was determined to make the most of it.

Cármen gave a hurried glance around her. Rose still remained invisible. It was very lonely there in the old garden, and the stillness seemed to be intensified by the low, soft buzzing of the bees. There was a tightness about her heart, and she felt a little faint. Her color had left her face and she was quite pale. She seated herself with a little sigh. But she realized that another rally was necessary, for the shakiness of Pem's voice had an unmistakable meaning. She could guess pretty well, no matter what his one question might be, in what direction it ultimately would lead, and she felt that she must check him before it was spoken. Her wits, however, were not in very good working order, and she presented the first thought that came into her mind—the thought, indeed, that had been uppermost in her mind all that day :

" The Señor soon will leave Mexico ? " she said.   She was aware even as these words were spoken that they served her purpose badly.   Pem perceived this too, and hastened to avail himself of the opening.   " And the Señorita will be glad when I am gone ? "

"Glad ?   No.   But everything must have an end, and the Señor no doubt now is tired of this land and will have pleasure in returning to his own.   He will have many lively stories to tell his friends about the savages whom he has seen in Mexico; and then presently he will forget Mexico and the savages, and will be busied again with his own concerns.   Is it not so ? "

" Is it the custom of Mexicans thus to forget friends who have shown them great kindness; or does the Señorita argue by contraries, and declare that because Mexicans are grateful there is no such virtue as gratitude among Americans ?   Does the Señorita truly in her heart believe that I shall forget the kindness that has been shown to me here, and the—and those who have shown it?"

"Ah, well, it is a little matter, not worth talking about," Cármen replied, uneasily. "No doubt some Americans have feelings of gratitude, and other virtues as well. But, as the Señor knows, I am not fond of Americans. I know too well the story of my own country. Yes, I know that I should not have spoken of this again," Cármen went on, answering the pained look on Pem's face, "but it is not my fault. The Señor should not have made me talk about Americans." This with a little air of defiance. "And least of all in this place. The Señor knows that this very convent was captured by his countrymen from mine? But does he remember that after the surrender, when he was asked to give up his ammunition, the General Anaya replied, ' Had I any ammunition, you would not be here?' Is not that the whole story of the war, told in a single word? Does the Señor wonder that I hate the Americans with all my heart?"

Pem was less disconcerted by this sally than he had been by the similar revival of dead issues at the Molino del Rey. He was fairly well convinced in his own mind that Cármen was saying not more than she meant in the abstract, perhaps; but, certainly, a good deal more than she meant in the concrete as applied to himself. It was his belief that she was forcing this new fighting of the old war as a rather desperate means of delivering herself from engaging in a new and more personal conflict. He also inferred from her adoption of a line of defence that he knew was distasteful to her that, like General Anaya, she was short of ammunition. Entertaining these convictions, he was disposed to press the attack vigorously.

"Let us not talk about Americans," he said. "Let us talk about one single American. Does the Señorita hate *me?*"

This sudden and very pointed question produced much the same effect as that of the unmasking of a heavy mortar battery. It threw the enemy into great confusion, and for a moment completely silenced the defending guns.

Cármen was not prepared for so sharp a shifting of the conversation from general to exceedingly personal grounds. She flushed again, and then again grew pale. She was silent for a very long while—at least so it seemed to Pem. Her head was reclining backward against the trellis-work of the arbor in a way that showed the beautiful lines of her throat. Her eyes were nearly closed, and almost wholly veiled by her long black lashes—that seemed still blacker by contrast with her pale cheeks. Her mouth was open a little, and her breath came and went irregularly. Her face was still; but as Pem waited for her answer, watching her closely, he saw an expression of resolve come into it. Then at last she spoke :

"I do hate you," she said, slowly and firmly. But as she spoke the words there was a drawing of the muscles of her face, as though she suffered bodily pain.

" Unearthed at last ! By Jove, Smith, I

had begun to think that you and the Señorita and Rose had fitted yourselves out with wings and flown away somewhere. I've been looking for you high and low, literally; for I've been up on the roof of the convent, and now I'm down here. Where is Rose? Doña Catalina said that you all three were here in the garden. Oh! there she comes now. Come! We're all waiting for you; it's time to start back to town."

Brown was of the opinion that he did not at all deserve the rating that Rose gave him, on the first convenient opportunity, for perpetrating this most untoward interruption. "How the dickens could I know they were spooning by themselves?" he asked. "I thought that you all three were together, of course." And although Rose, who took the matter a good deal to heart, replied that this "was just like him," she could not but accept this reasonable excuse.

On Pem and Cármen the effects of the interruption were different. Whatever her more considerate opinion might be, Cármen's first feeling certainly was that of relief. She had fired the shot that she had nerved herself to fire, and the diversion had come just in time to check the reply of the enemy and to cover her orderly retreat.

Pem, realizing that the situation was critical, was thoroughly indignant. He wanted to punch Brown's head. Fortunately no opportunity offered for this practical expression of his wrath, and by the time that he got back to town he had cooled down a little. But he was so grumpy on the return journey, and looked so thoroughly uncomfortable, that the motherly Doña Catalina expressed grave concern when she bade him good-by and frankly asked him—with the freedom that is permissible in Spanish—if anything that he had eaten at breakfast had disagreed with him ? And being only half-convinced by his disclaimer, she advised him to take a tumblerful of hot water with a dash of tequila in it as soon as he got home.

VII.

THE STORMING OF CHAPULTEPEC.

WHEN Pem, a few days later, had recovered his composure sufficiently to give Rose a circumstantial account of the Churubusco battle, that very hopeful young person took her usual cheerful view of what some people might have considered a desperate situation.

"It couldn't have been better if we'd planned it all in advance," she said. "Even Van's interruption was just what was wanted, and I shall tell the poor boy that I am sorry I scolded him so for it; I will, indeed.

"Don't you see," she went on—for Pem certainly did not look much like a person who saw anything of an encouraging nature anywhere—"don't you see what a fix she's got herself into by saying a great deal more than she meant to? It's all as plain as possible. She made up her mind some time ago, just as I told you, that she would fight you off, because she was afraid she would fall in love with you; which meant that she really had begun to fall in love with you and didn't know it—or that she knew it and wouldn't tell herself about it. You can't understand that, I suppose; but any woman can. And then you succeeded in getting her off that way, and began to say things to her; and she got worried, and scared, and lost her wits a little, and hit ever so much harder than she really meant to. She never would have brought up the war again, I'm sure, if she hadn't felt herself to be in a corner and quite desperate. When you suddenly twisted things round on her that way, her first thought, of course, was to tell you that she didn't hate you at all. And then she saw that wouldn't do, for it would give you a chance to go right ahead and ask her if she loved you. And then she thought things over and came to the conclusion—you must

always remember what a horrid time she had
with that dreadful old husband, and how firmly she has made up her mind never to marry
again—and then, I say, she came to the conclusion that the only thing to do was to break
things off short, and have done with it. So
she said that she hated you."

"Well, that is only another way of telling
all that I have told you, Mrs. Brown."

"It is not what you told at all; for you
told it as though you thought that she meant
it, and I know that she didn't. She only
meant to mean it, that's all."

"Aren't we dropping into metaphysics a
little?" Pem asked, drearily. "I don't see
that much comfort is to be had from such a
finely drawn distinction as that is. Meaning
a thing, and meaning to mean a thing, strike
me as convertible terms. Don't they you?"

"If a man used them, I suppose they would
not have much difference; but when a woman
uses them, they have all the difference in the
world. When a woman really means a thing
she means it—that is, of course, for the time

being. Naturally, things happen sometimes to make her change her mind. But when she only means to mean a thing, she does not really, in the depths of her heart, mean it at all. She only thinks that she ought to, you know. And in the case of Cármen," Rose went on, becoming practical, much to Pem's relief—for his masculine mind very imperfectly grasped this line of highly abstract feminine reasoning—" it is perfectly clear that she only said she hated you because she has this foolish notion in her head about not getting married, and was ready to say anything at the moment that would stop you from finding out that she really loves you. For she does love you now, Mr. Smith ; and, what is more, she knows it herself."

" But if she won't admit that she loves me, and if she continues to hold me off in this way, I don't see that any good can come of it. It has been very kind of you, Mrs. Brown, to help me as you have done, and to be so sympathetic and good to me, and I am as grateful to you as I can be. But I think that I'll give up now. It isn't fair, you know, to trouble her any more when it is so clear that she wants me to keep away from her. So I think that to-morrow I'll go up to Guanajuato—it was there that I first saw her, you know—and I—I should like to go once more to the Presa, where we had our first walk together. And then I'll go on north. I'd be rather poor company, so I don't mind leaving the party. And I think that I will take a long journey somewhere. I've been wanting for some time to go into Central Africa : it must be a very interesting country, from what I've read about it. And if I should happen to die of the coast-fever, or get bowled over in a fight, or something of that sort, you know, it might be just as well. And some time or other you will see her again, very likely; and then you'll tell her that I really did think a good deal of her, won't you ? And if she——"

" Mr. Smith," said Rose, with severity, " you will please stop right there. What you are to do to-morrow is not to go to Guanajuato, and from there to a grave in Central Africa. You are going with the rest of us to Chapultepec—and you are going to try again!"

" But what chance will I have to try again ? You don't suppose for a moment, do you, that Cármen will be of the party ? She will know that I will be with the rest of you, or, at least, she will expect me to be, and of course she will stay at home."

" No," said Rose, decidedly; " she will not stay at home. During the past few days she has been thinking things over and has been very miserable. Violet saw her yesterday, and said that she looked wretchedly. And she said that Cármen talked to her for nearly two hours about the way we live at home and about Violet's own life, and said things about the impossibility of Mexicans and Americans marrying, seemingly to give Violet a chance to say how happy her marriage with Mr. Mauve had been. And she asked if it wasn't true that all the Americans wanted to make war again on Mexico, and if

they were not talking about it all the time
and getting ready for it, and seemed very
much astonished when Violet told her that the
majority of Americans knew very little more
about Mexico than that there was such a
country in existence, and that they had no
more notion of making war against it than of
making war against the moon. And what
she knows now about the happy life that
Violet has led after being married to an
American, together with what she herself had
been thinking about the probability that her
own dismal marriage wasn't a fair sample of
married life at all, I'm sure has put her mind
into a very unsettled state all around. What
you must do now is to finish unsettling
it, and then settle it for her once and for all.
She certainly will give you the chance. I
think that I have not told you yet that she
told Violet that she was going to Chapultepec?"

"Oh, Mrs. Brown! How could you keep
that back until the very last ?"

"So, will you go to Chapultepec too, Mr.

Smith ; or do you still insist upon Central Africa and a lonely grave ? "

The expedition to Chapultepec was in the nature of a farewell, for on the ensuing day the Americans were to leave the City of Mexico for their visit to the Carmine *hacienda* on Lake Cuitzeo.   If they returned to the capital it would be only for a night on their way northward ; and there was a possibility that they might take the train for the north at Celaya, and so not return to the capital at all.   They were pretty dismal over the prospect of home-going, for a very warm love of Mexico had taken possession of all their hearts.   Even Mrs. Gamboge, while firmly of the opinion that there was something radically wrong in a country that countenanced hard pillows and employed men as chambermaids, admitted that this journey into Mexico was the pleasantest journey that she had ever made.

And they all were very grateful to the Mexican friends who had done so much to

make their stay in the capital delightful.
The several interpreters of the party were
kept busy that afternoon, as they walked in
the beautiful park of Chapultepec, in rendering into Spanish hearty words of thanks, and
into English courteous disclaimers of obliga-
tion conferred. The pleasure had been all
on their side, said their Mexican friends. Nor
was this interchange of international amen-
ities ended when they passed out from beneath
the long, slanting shadows of the great *ahue-
huetes*—the moss-draped trees which were old
four centuries ago, before ever the Spaniards
came into the land—and slowly walked up the
winding way to the height on which the
castle stands.

Pem had been shocked when he first saw
Cármen's face that afternoon. The lines
were drawn as though with illness, and she
seemed older by a full year than when he last
had seen her. He saw, too, that the spring
had gone out of her step, and an air of lan-
guor hung over her that she made no effort
to throw off. She did not seek to evade

him, but as they walked together she managed always to keep near her aunt ; and her
talk, conforming to her actions, was languid
and dull. The only sign of good hope that
he could perceive was that gradually a little
color came into her face and a little brightness into her eyes.

As they went up the terraced road to the
castle, catching lovely glimpses of the valley
out between the trees, Pem. walked slowly,
that they might drop behind the rest and be
alone. Once or twice he stopped, calling her
attention to the view. His tactics were not
successful ; for as soon as the space between
themselves and the others became appreciable
she hastened her steps, and the chance that
he thought he had secured was lost. Yet he
marked a little hesitancy in her manner each
time this manœuvre was executed that seemed
to imply a disposition on her part, possibly all
the stronger because it was thus checked, to
grant him the opportunity to speak that he
desired. Once, or twice even, she herself lin-
gered in the way and seemed about to speak ;

and then moved quickly forward, holding her peace.

Pem would have been glad of the chance to take counsel of Rose at this juncture, for he was at a loss to determine whether these curious signs promised good or boded ill. This young gentleman from Philadelphia was not very wise in the ways of women; but even had he been far wiser than he was, Cármen's curious conduct very well might have puzzled him.

As they came out upon the eastern terrace the glorious sunset view, a reflected splendor in the east, burst upon them—one of the great sunset views of the world.

Below them, at the foot of the sharp, craggy descent, and surrounded by the trees of the eastern park, lay the tiny lake that Carlotta caused to be made while she played for a little space her part of empress here in the castle. To the right lay Tacubaya, a cluster of low, square houses embowered in trees, on a long, sloping hill-side; and beyond Tacubaya rose the blue encircling wall of mountains, culminating in the great solemn mass of Ajusco, that shuts in the valley on the south. To the left lay the city, with its tall church towers rising high above the houses, and its many domes, covered with glazed tiles, flashing in the last rays of the sun ; and, farther on, the church of Guadalupe stood out against the hazy lines of the mountains of Teypeyac, and on Lake Tezcuco shimmered a soft light. Right in front, the trees of the park merged into other trees beyond its limits; and the great valley, dotted with gray houses, and gray church towers, and green remnants of ancient forests, and broad green meadows, stretched away for miles and miles eastward ; and in the midst of it the waters of Lake Chalco shone as though on fire. And beyond all, against the limit of the eastern sky, towered the two great volcanoes—masses of gold and crimson clouds above them, and a rich rosy light resting upon their crest-coverings of eternal snow.

Cármen and Pem had stopped a little behind the others ; and when Don Antonio suggested a slight change of position, she took a step or two and then stood still.   The others moved a little to the left.   Pem moved a little to the right; and Cármen, following him, seated herself upon a low wall.   The little color that had come into her cheeks in the park had left them now; but her eyes had brightened curiously.   Presently they heard Don Antonio advise a move to the roof of the castle: this hospitable Mexican seemed to regard the sunset as an entertainment that he himself had provided for the pleasure of his American friends, and wished to make sure that they got the full benefit of it.   Pem looked inquiringly at Cármen; but her gaze was fixed upon the distant mountains, and she made no sign of moving.   Then the sound of footsteps and voices died away; and so, at last, they were alone.

Cármen had leaned her head back against the stone wall—just as she had sat that day at Churubusco—and was looking out dreamily across the valley.   For the time being she appeared to be quite unconscious of the fact of Mr. Pemberton Logan Smith's existence. Although the situation was precisely that which for two hours past he had been seeking to accomplish, Pem found it, now that it was secured, a trifle embarrassing. Cármen's manner did not at all invite the utterance of the words which he so earnestly desired to speak; but the longer that the silence continued the more he found his nerves going wrong. It was rather at random that he spoke at last.

"The great mountain to the left is called the White Woman, I am told, Señorita. It is a dismal fancy, this of a dead woman lying enshrouded in the snow."

Cármen gave a little sigh as she roused herself. "The Señor does not know the story," she answered, absently. "The White Woman is not dead. Far down beneath the snow-covering the fires of her life burn hotly. She sleeps; and the great mountain beside her is her lover, who wakens her with his kiss. This is the foolish story that the common people tell. The Mexicans are very silly, very superstitious, very stupid — as the Señor knows."

Cármen uttered her comments upon the legend and upon her fellow - countrymen hastily and nervously, as though seeking to divert attention from the folk-story itself— a story that she had known, of course, all her life, and that she had told in sheer absence of mind.

" Is it not possible, Señorita," Pem replied, ignoring that portion of her speech that she had added precisely for the purpose of diverting him from what she perceived to be a dangerous line of investigation, "that this is not a foolish story, but a wise allegory ?   May it not sometimes happen that real women seek to hide with snow the warm love that is in their hearts ? I am not speaking lightly, Señorita.   I should be very glad to believe that this story has a deep meaning within it ; that it is not a mere foolish fancy, but a beautiful and eternal truth."   And then he added, speaking very gently, " Will not the Señorita tell me that this may be true ? "

Cármen was silent for a moment, and when she spoke there was a grave, solemn tone in her voice that struck a chill into Pem's heart.

"Yes, Señor," she said ; "it *is* true. It is true now and it has been true always. Since the world began there must always have been some women whose fate it was that their love thus should be chilled upon its surface and so hidden ; and believe me, Señor"—and a certain wistfulness of expression came into Cármen's face as she spoke—"such hidden love as this perhaps may be stronger than the love that is felt and known."

Cármen was silent for a moment, but there was something in her manner that made Pem refrain from speech. Then, still speaking in the same chill, solemn tone, and very slowly, she went on :

"I know what you mean, Señor. I am not a young girl. I have been in the world, and I understand. You do me the honor to love me, and to want my love in return. But this may not be—not, that is, in the way that you desire. I cannot tell you the story of my life. There are some things in it that I have not told even to the good father to whom I confess. Perhaps this has been a sin ; but sometimes I think that this rule of our Church which commands us to lay bare our hearts to men, though the men are God's ministers, is not a good rule. It is a great presumption for me to cherish such a thought, but I cannot help it. I have told my sorrows to the God who made me, and who in his wisdom has made my life sad ; not to his mother, nor to his saints, you understand, but to him.

" And what I have told only to God I cannot tell even to you. But you may know at least that my life has been very, very bitter since the time that—that I was sold. I really was sold, Señor ; and I had not even the poor consolation which is given to some unhappy, lost women—but less unhappy and less hopelessly lost than I am—of selling myself. It was as though I had been put in a market-place like a horse or a cow, and for my poor beauty's sake I was bought! Of the time that came afterward I cannot speak, I cannot bear even to think "—Cármen shuddered as she spoke and her face flushed with shame and anger—" but yet I cannot drive the horror of it from my thoughts. And then, at last—to others it seemed very soon, but not to me—the God who had brought this bitter sorrow upon me gave me a little help, for my owner died. It had been better far that I had died too, for I was dead to peace, to hope; my life was ended at a time when for most women life has just begun."

Again Cármen was silent for a little space, and then she said: "Now you will understand, Señor, why it is that I tell you that the story of the White Woman yonder is true; for I myself, a living woman, know that whatever there may be of warm love in my heart must remain forever buried deep beneath the snow."

Pem's eyes had tears in them as Cármen ceased to speak. Once or twice he had put out his hand to her, but she had motioned it away. When she had made an end he spoke eagerly; and while his voice was husky and uncertain, its tone was firm.

" Cármen, Carmencita," he said, "your sorrows have been very heavy and hard to bear, but may not the time have come, at last, when in place of sorrow you shall have happiness ? Is it too much for me to offer you this hope ? But in my love—my love is very strong, Carmencita; far stronger now that I know how grievous your life has been—I do not dare too greatly when I promise you shelter and great tenderness; and so may come to you peace and rest. And remember," he went on quickly, checking her rising speech, "that my happiness for all my life rests now upon your answer. Love is a very selfish passion, otherwise I would not think, after what you have told me, of my own happiness at all. But I do think of it, though less than of yours. I know that without you my life will be hopeless and worthless. I believe that with me, away from all those things which will not permit you to forget—

in a new life that will make forgetfulness easy, and that will give you the breadth and the freedom that I know you need and wish —happiness is in store for you. Think, think of all this before you tell me that you will live on despairingly, and that into my life also you will bring despair."

Cármen sat motionless. Through her half-closed eyes she looked out upon the fading sunset. The golden gleams no longer were in the sky now, and the crimson had faded into a soft rose-color. On the snow-peaks rested a deep violet tint, and the White Woman shone ghost-like through a purple haze.

"Señor," she said at last, "it may not be. What you have told me of the life that I could live with you I know in my heart is truth. I know that among your people I should find what I long for, and what I cannot find among my own. I have longed with all my heart's strength for the life that you offer me; and I have longed for it far more since I have known you. And I do love you——" Pem started forward, but Cármen restrained him by a motion of her hand. " I love you so well that I cannot consent to accept my happiness at such a cost to you. After the shame that has been put upon me I feel that I am not fit to be your—your wife; I am not fit to be the wife of any honest man. Could you but know !"

Cármen shuddered again, and her voice dropped low. Then, in a moment, she went on: " This is an old, old world, Señor, and it seems to me that some day it must of itself fall to pieces, so heavy is the load of sorrow and suffering and shame that it carries. But we who are of it must bear with it, and must bear our own part in it, stayed by such hope of another and a better world as God in his goodness may put into our hearts. Sometimes I think that the talk about God's goodness is only a fond delusion, invented by men to save themselves wholly from despair. But I fight against this thought, for if it once fairly possessed my soul I know that I should go mad. And what matters when all is sorrow, one sorrow more or less ?   I have borne much and of my suffering no good has come. What I bear now in refusing the life that you offer me I can bear gladly, for I know that I am bringing good to you.   So this is the end.

"See, the dark shadows are falling upon the White Woman.   The fire is there, but it is, it must be, covered with eternal snow. Hark ! Don Antonio is calling us.   We must go to him."

"Cármen," said Pem, speaking resolutely and quickly, " I will not take this answer.   I command you not to wreck both of our lives when for both of us happiness is within easy reach.   I love you, and so I am your servant ; but you own your love for me, and so I am your master.   By the right that this love gives me I lay on you my command—accept my love, and with it the life that I offer you !"

"Señor—I—I—how can I answer ?   At least—let me think.   Give me a little time."

Voices and footsteps were near at hand. Pem had only a moment left.   " You shall have time to think. To-morrow we go to the *hacienda.* We shall be there a week ; longer, perhaps. Very well, I give you till my return to think. But remember, my order has been given, and it must be obeyed ! "

"It was much finer, the view from the tower of the castle, Señor; why did you linger here ? " Don Antonio asked, politely, but in the slightly injured tone of one who, having provided a feast, feels that a guest is not doing justice to it.

" You must forgive me, Don Antonio, but the Señorita, your niece, as we turned to follow you, had a narrow escape from a fall here at this broken space in the parapet. It was a great danger, and the shock unnerved her. See, she still is pale. But she is recovering now, and we were about to go in search of you when we heard you call."

Cármen, no doubt, was grateful to Pem for this somewhat stirring flight of fancy; but it involved them both subsequently in a rather trying exercise of their respective imaginations, for the entire party insisted upon hearing the minutest details of the adventure told.   Only Rose refrained from questioning. She had not much faith in the parapet story, but she did have her own ideas, and reserved her questions accordingly.   But what really had happened, beyond the bare fact that that afternoon on the heights of Chapultepec had marked a turning-point in the campaign, Rose never knew.

VIII.

THE CONQUEST OF MEXICO.

SEÑOR CARMINE'S hospitality, being put to a practical test by the arrival at his *hacienda* of the entire American party, proved to be as boundless in fact as it had been boundless in promise. His only regret was that the party had not been organized on a larger scale. Jaune and Van, indeed, found his pressing questions as to why the surviving parents of their respective wives had not come with them a trifle embarrassing.

The Señora Carmine—or Mrs. Carmine, as, with lingering memories of her early life at Fort Leavenworth, she preferred to be styled—was equally instant, and far more voluble, in her expressions of welcome and general good-will. She was a stout, jolly woman of eight-and-forty, or thereabouts, with just a suggestion of brogue in her English and Spanish, and with a heart that seemed to be as big as she herself was broad. Rowney Mauve found her at once shocking and delightful, and had the wisdom to congratulate himself upon the fact that his feelings toward his mother-in-law could be of this mixed sort. From Violet's report of her he had expected that things would be a good deal worse.

In point of fact, all of the Americans had dreaded this visit a little. It is one thing to associate somewhat formally with foreigners in a city, and it is quite another thing to be projected into close and intimate association with a foreign family in its own home. Mrs. Gamboge, in whose character adaptability was not an especially prominent trait, frankly admitted that she wished that the visit were well over; and in this wish Mr. Gamboge, who took a warm interest in his own personal comfort and was impressed by a prophetic conviction that this was one of the occasions when his personal comfort would have to be sacrificed, heartily sympathized. Mr. Mangan Brown had his own private doubts as to how things would work out ; but he went at the matter cheerfully, and comforted himself with the conviction that, after all, a fortnight is not a very important part of a lifetime. The younger members of the party were disposed to regard the visit in the light of a very original frolic, and to get as much fun out of it as possible.

Violet, of course, was in a condition of enthusiastic delight that she manifested in her own vigorous fashion, completely exhausting Rowney Mauve during the first two or three days by trotting him about, on foot and on horseback, to see the various places and people and things on the *hacienda* especially beloved by her. And when Rowney, who was a capital horseman, got the better of the bucking pony, Violet's pride in him was unbounded. This equine victory of Rowney's had the further good result of settling him firmly in the Carmine family heart.

" Ah ! he can ride," said Señor Carmine, with the same complacent air that an American father would say of his daughter's husband: "He is worth a solid half-million; he is a consistent church-member, and he belongs to one of the best families in the State!"

But none of the doubts which disturbed the minds of the American visitors disturbed the minds of their Mexican hosts. Self-consciousness is not a characteristic of the kindly Spanish-American race. With a frank cordiality Señor Carmine welcomed these strangers within his gates; and as he was very glad to see them his guests, he did not for a moment imagine that they could be anything else than glad too. In a general way he knew that their customs must be unlike his, and he expected some manifestations of this difference which would seem to him strange. Americans were curious creatures. Had he not married one, and did he not know? It was a cardinal belief with Señor Carmine that his wife, the Señora Brígida O'Jara de Carmine—the descendant, as she herself had assured him, of a line of Irish kings, and the daughter of a prominent citizen of Fort Leavenworth — was a shining example of the grace, the elegance, and the refinement of the Americans of the North.   It surprised him a good deal to find how, in certain ways, the American ladies now his guests differed from this his standard of American ladyhood.

As for the Señora, this access of American society caused her to renew her youth like the eagles.   It was her desire to make the house and the household, for the time being, as American as possible.   She arranged her guest-chambers in the fashion, as nearly as she could remember it, of the aristocratic hotel in Kansas City that her father had taken her to for a week, five and twenty years before.   She introduced substantial breakfasts at eight o'clock; and Señor Carmine, eating for politeness' sake, nearly ruined his digestion by his enforced abandonment of his morning bread and chocolate.

On the evening that the Americans arrived, this hospitable lady announced that " it 'u'd be after makin' them feel more home-like, sure, to play some American games," and added, after a moment's reflection, "How 'u'd yees like 'Copenhagen,' now?" And in spite of Violet's protests, Mrs. Carmine organized the game instantly, and "chose" Mr. Mangan Brown and kissed him with a hearty smack that was the very embodiment of cheery hospitality. And both Señor Carmine and Mrs. Gamboge were rather shocked, and very nervous over it, when Señor Carmine, acting under his wife's orders, in accordance with the rules of elegant society in Fort Leavenworth, "chose" and kissed the eldest lady among his guests.

Señor Carmine felt called upon to explain through Violet that this cordial freedom was not in accordance with Mexican customs, which very emphatically was the truth. "But while our house is honored by the presence of Americans," he added, "we desire to make our ways like theirs." Even Mr. Gamboge, after this friendly speech, was not so lacking in tact as to suggest that their host be informed that "Copenhagen" was not an ordinary form of evening amusement in all classes of society in New York.

However, in private, Violet took upon herself the task of enlightening her mother in the premises. The Señora was a good deal cut up about it.

" To think how times has changed since I was a gurrl, Violet dear! We all uv us, from the Mejor down, was great hands for kissin'-games in the old days at the Foort; an' moighty good fun 'twas, too. Your mother's after feelin' that she's an old woman, sure," ruefully said the descendant of the royal house of O'Jara. But she accepted her daughter's advice in good part, and among the various modes of entertainment which she thereafter devised for the benefit of her guests " kissing-games " did not reappear.

To Rose the most distinctive feature of the visit was the arrangement of her bedchamber. The Señora's memory of the hotel in Kansas City had not been very clear. In fact, it consisted principally of rocking-chairs. As it is a matter of pride with Mexican·

housewives to have as many chairs as possible in a room, the Señora had sent a liberal order for rocking-chairs to the City of Mexico as soon as the coming of the Americans had been arranged.

"It's a little horrifying, somehow, Van, don't you think," Rose said, "to see all those six rocking-chairs in a row that way? It's like ghosts and skeletons, you know." Brown failed to see where the ghostliness and skeleton-likeness came in; but he was accustomed to having Rose discover unexpected resemblances, and took the matter easily.

"Of course the two little beds are all right," she went on, "for that's the regular Mexican custom; but I wish they hadn't put them at opposite ends of the room—it's such a very big room, you see."

"Big enough for a town-hall, up in our part of the world," Van assented.

"But suppose I'm taken sick, or something frightens me in the night; what am I to do?"

"You might have your shoes handy, and

shy them at me. You wouldn't be likely to throw straight enough to hit me; but I'd hear things banging about, and wake up in time to rescue you."

"Don't be foolish, Van; I'm really in earnest. It is dreadful to be so far away in the dark. And—why, Van, there isn't any slop-bucket, and there's only one towel! And it can't be because they're poor, or anything like that, for they're not; and the basin and the pitcher are perfectly beautiful French china, good enough for bric-à-brac. Don't you think it very strange? Oh! who's that?"

Van himself was a little startled, for a door at the end of the room opened and a nice-looking old woman placidly walked through the apartment—smiling in a friendly way at them—and passed out by one of the doors opening on the corridor, bidding them as she departed, an affable good-night. Neither Rose nor Van was exactly in costume for receiving even transient visitors.

Brown went to close the door through

which the old woman had entered. " Why, it's a chapel ! " he said. " She must have been in there saying her prayers. And I don't see what we are going to do about ventilation," he continued, as he examined the doors opening on the corridor. " These things are solid wood, three inches thick. If we shut them, we won't have any fresh air at all ; and if we leave them open, anybody can see in. The Mexicans seem to have very extraordinary notions of privacy, any-way."

" I don't like it at all," said Rose. " And with all these old women marching about— but she seemed a nice sort of old woman, I must say—and these open doors, and all, I'm quite nervous. You'd better shut them all tight, Van. It is such a big room that the air won't be very bad."

But Brown left the door in the corner open, and the first thing that he knew in the morning he was waking up and finding a serving-man gravely entering with an earthen jar of fresh water. The man said good-morning, in a matter-of-fact way, and asked—as far as Brown could make out—if the Señor and Señora had rested well, and if there was anything else that he could bring them.

Violet seemed rather surprised when Rose, in a delicate way, lodged a remonstrance against these intrusions.

"Oh, you needn't mind them," she said. "Old Margarita always goes into the oratory at night to say her prayers—she is a dear old thing. And if Juan doesn't bring you fresh water in the morning, and see if you want anything, what are you going to do?"

Rose did not feel at liberty to speak about the one towel. She drew on her private stock. At the end of a week the one towel was removed, and a clean towel was put in its place. They were very elegant, in their way, these solitary towels; of beautiful linen, and ornamented with a good deal of handsome embroidery. Rose never quite succeeded in making up her mind as to whether they really were intended for use, or simply were fitting accessories to the bric-à-brac basin and pitcher.

In regard to the slop-bucket, Violet settled the matter promptly. " Just empty your basin out over the edge of the corridor," she said. " That's the way we always do, you know." And that was the way they did.

Another peculiarity of the household that struck the Americans forcibly was that at meals the women were given their food after the men. The first portion went to Mr. Mangan Brown, the next to Mr. Gamboge, and then the younger men, in turn, received their portions. After this the women, beginning with Mrs. Gamboge, were served. It made one feel like living in the Middle Ages, Rose said.

But with all the oddities and peculiarities of domestic life which they encountered, the underlying kindliness and hearty hospitality of their entertainers made the Americans feel thoroughly sorry when the fortnight came to an end. It was a matter of some doubt, indeed, as to whether they would be permitted to leave at the end of this very short visit. Señor Carmine had counted upon having them with him for several months, he assured them; why could they not stay on? The summer was such a lovely season on the plateau—never hot, never cold; and all manner of delicious fruit to be gathered freshly every day.   Why should they not remain?

But Señor Carmine yielded to the inevitable, and aided his wife in devising and arranging stores of all manner of good things to eat and to drink for his departing guests to take with them for sustenance by the way. From the quantities of food provided for this purpose, anybody but a Mexican would have inferred that the party was about setting forth to cross an exceedingly wide desert; instead of upon a comfortable journey of eight hours by rail, with very fair opportunities for sustaining life by stops at two reasonably good eating-stations.

The one member of the party who really was glad to leave the *hacienda* was Mr. Pemberton Logan Smith.   Pem never had known two weeks so long as these two weeks had been. He had done his best to be as cheerful as possible, for he was a well-bred young man, with strong convictions in regard to the impropriety of exhibiting publicly his private griefs; but in spite of his best efforts he had not been wholly successful, so very much depended upon that answer which he was to receive when the two weeks were at an end. He had played a masterful part that day at Chapultepec, but would he be able to keep on playing it? Cármen loved him — she admitted it; but could he force her to give him her love? These were the questions which constantly were in his mind, constantly tormenting him with their varying answers and consequent shiftings from hopeful elation to desolating doubts and fears. Even to have desolation set in for a permanency was better, he thought, than that this racking uncertainty should endure. And so he was very glad when at last his face was set once more toward certainty and the City of Mexico.

Although the train did not arrive at the Colonia Station until after eight o'clock at night, Don Antonio was on hand to meet them, and had a little procession of carriages in readiness for their conveyance to their hotel. No one would have been surprised had he brought along a brass band. Had he happened to think of it, very likely he would.

He had planned one more expedition for them, he said ; and hastened to add, fearing that the question of lack of time would be raised, that it was a very little one. It was only to go once more to the shrine of Guadalupe. They had been there once, but he feared that they had not drunk of the water of the Holy Well. Did they know that whoever drank of this water needs must return—no matter how far away they might stray into the world—to drink again ? Therefore they must come with him and drink : so would he have assurance that they all would return.

Of course, an invitation of this gracious

sort could not be refused; and so it was decided to defer the start northward for yet another day, and to go to Guadalupe on the following afternoon. Pem was well pleased with this arrangement, and especially with the fact, mentioned by Don Antonio incidentally, that it was to his niece that he owed the suggestion of assuring in this way the return of their American friends. Pem could not but believe that herein was ground for hope.

But from Cármen's face, when they all met the next afternoon in the Plaza, he could make nothing: her eyes were downcast, and her lips were firm. But it comforted him to see that the wearied, pained look, that had shocked him so when they last met at Chapultepec, had disappeared. During the short ride on the tramway she sat nearly opposite to him in the car, her eyes still cast down. But through the veil of her dark lashes he felt that she was looking at him earnestly.

As the church already had been visited,

there was nothing to detain them from the immediate object of their pilgrimage. Therefore Don Antonio, gallantly escorting Mrs. Gamboge, led the way directly across the pretty *plazuela*, past the old parish church and so to the beautiful little chapel— the masterpiece of the architect Guerrero y Torres—that covers the Holy Well.

With something of the serious air of one who administers a religious rite, Don Antonio dipped up the water through the iron grating and served it to his American friends. As Pem drank, Cármen for an instant looked full upon him. It was a strange look : but again Pem believed that he had a right to hope.

When the ceremony was ended they mounted the stone stairway that winds up the hill-side, to take a last look at the sun-set light upon the snow mountains.

"Not a last look," Don Antonio correctingly interposed. "You have drunk of the water of the Holy Well."

In the Mexican fashion the gentlemen

offered their hands to the ladies to assist them in the ascent. Pem gave his hand to Cármen; hers was very cold, and it trembled as it touched his.

Where the stairways from the opposite sides of the hill unite, on the little plateau before the stone screen, they paused to rest; and when the party moved on, passing beyond the screen, Pem took Cármen's hand, as though to follow, but gently detained her. He felt her hand tremble again. She withdrew it from his, and in obedience to his gesture seated herself beside him upon the stone bench. And so once more they were alone at sunset.

But now that the moment for which Pem had longed so earnestly had come, his fears entirely overmastered his hopes, and he did not dare to speak. He knew that this hour would decide his life for him. He remembered all that Cármen had urged to make clear to him that while she loved him she could not give him her love; he remembered how little substantial ground she had given

him that day for believing that the conclusion which she had arrived at deliberately, and deliberately had stated a fortnight
before, was to be reversed. And as these
dreary thoughts possessed him, hope slipped
farther and farther away from his heart.

Cármen sat silently beside him. Her
open hand rested upon the stone bench, not
far from his, but he had not the courage to
take it. Her eyes were turned eastward
toward the snow mountains. High above
the snow-capped peaks was a glory of red
and golden cloud, but the mountains below
were cold and colorless. To Pem's mind
the White Woman seemed more than ever
a dead, cold woman, half hidden beneath her
shroud of snow. And as this dreary thought
came into his mind, linking itself with the
sorrowful thoughts already there, and by an
allegory making the sorrow of them still more
keen, there came from his lips a sob. Doubt-
less there is no sound more pathetic than the
sob of a strong man.

And then Pem felt a soft hand, not cold,

but warm, in his; and at that instant a shifting of the clouds changed the current of the sunlight, and the White Woman was lit up by a ruddy, life-giving glow.

Pem's heart bounded. He raised his head, and his eyes met Cármen's — looking full at him now, bright through tears and full of love.

" Señor, Señor mio," said Cármen, as they rose at last from the stone bench, yet still looked eastward on the splendor of gold and crimson clouds and crimsoned snow, " it was here in Guadalupe Hidalgo that the treaty of peace between the conquered Mexicans and the conquering Americans was signed."

THE END.